PRAISE FOR BONDED LOVE

"Bonded love presents a balanced approach to real-life issues through scripture and fresh, practical life experiences. This profoundly understandable book provides insight into the accessibility of God's continuous in-reach with warm freshness. The document is written with balanced language, wit, humor, and illuminating love."

Dr. Clifford A. Jones, Sr., Senior Pastor Friendship Missionary Baptist Church, Charlotte, NC

"The Reverend Dr. Damone Paul Johnson has tapped into the pathos and complexity of human relationships through a biblical lens. This work is particularly relevant and needed in this age where relationships have been strained and fractured due to social distancing. You can feel Dr. Johnson's passion and personal experiences come glaring through in a refreshing way that makes Bonded Love come alive!"

Rev. Reginald Lee Bachus, President
The 400 Foundation, Inc.

"What a read! This intriguing, inspiring, and forthright book is evidence of the Bible made plain in our lives. The writer provokes you to realize how God's Word is still applicable."

Rev. Dr. James R Banks II
Pastor, Faith Baptist Church, Buffalo, NY
President, Empire Baptist Missionary Convention
Congress of Christian Education

"A long-needed message of LOVE and application that calls for 'cooperation' versus 'competition' in regard to human relationships. True sermons of LOVE."
Dr. Thomas L. Brown, Sr.
Ebenezer Baptist Church
Indianapolis, Indiana

"Practical and powerful- *Bonded love* is an insensible tool for those that are seeking balance in their relationships. This book takes an in-depth look at the heartache of life's relationships and offers solid practical solutions. Be prepared for a life-changing experience."
Rev. Raphael D. Montgomery
Mt. Calvary Missionary Baptist Church
Baytown, TX

"Dr. Johnson, in this work, presents an excellent series of messages that provide hope and healing for individuals experiencing the trauma caused by real-life situations and flawed relationships. Johnson emphasizes that hope and healing are found in experiencing the awesome power of love from an omnibenevolent God. This book is one more magnificent installment of the life-giving word of God, which is a balm in Gilead that heals the sin-sick soul. A must-read for those who are wounded and hurt -- those who stand in need of hope and healing."
Dr. Edward O. Williamson, Pastor-Teacher
Bethel Baptist Church of White Plains, NY
Dean/State Director, Empire Baptist Missionary Convention Congress of Christian Education

"Even through shattered experiences and unmet expectations, we can encounter the unyielding purposeful love of God. God's pure love illuminates beyond our past hurts, fears, and brokenness. The text is a practical, insightful, and refreshing affirmation of hope and healing through the Word of God. Whether you are married or single, this is a must-read."

We must remain committed and prayerful.
Rev. Dr. Brianna K. Parker
CEO, Black Millennial Café, LLC

BONDED *Love*

How God's Love Shines
Through Imperfect
Relationships

Damone Paul Johnson

"Dr. Johnson has captured in this book the essence of what God intends for each of us. *Bonded Love* speaks to Christ concern for us to have lasting, loving relationships that exceed the norm. Dr. Johnson is to be commended for capturing the essential call of the Gospel message that God is love and love creates an atmosphere for authentic relationship. I'm in awe at what God is going to do with this book. Congratulations Dr. Johnson and I endorse this effort."

Rev. Dr. Carl L. Washington, Jr., Senior Pastor
New Mount Zion Baptist Church, Harlem, NY
President, Empire Baptist Missionary Convention

DEDICATION

I dedicate this book to the love of my life, Lady Angela. We are bonded by love.

CONTENTS

FOREWORD

Those of us who were lovers of music will never forget when Damone P. Johnson arrived on the campus of Fisk University in Nashville. He was, for the most part, a quiet and unassuming college freshman who had made his way from Indiana to Tennessee. But when he sat at the piano to accompany the Gospel Choir, and later the Gospel Group a few of us had formed while students, his musicianship became a campus-wide topic of conversation. For some, that was all they knew of the one we simply called Damone. But over the years that ensued thereafter, we have learned that "an accomplished musician" is just a piece of the comprehensive puzzle that makes Damone Johnson who he is.

I am blessed that since our days at Fisk, I have come to know him likewise as an anointed Man of God, a preacher of the Gospel of Jesus Christ, a pastor who loves the flock of God over which he serves as shepherd, a denominational leader, who serves with integrity and now, through Bonded Love, we all get to know him as the author of this manuscript, bringing us a series of messages that helps us to understand how the love of God shines through even in the most challenging of human relationships. These twelve chapters help us to appreciate the leadership of this brother who has experienced the love of God on so many levels throughout his own life's journey. From early childhood adoption through countless other life experiences, God's love has shown him how no circumstance or situation can separate us from the love to which we have been bonded.

To be sure, the word-picture alone speaks volumes. BONDED is the depiction Johnson has been led to use. This is a love that is attached, fused, united to us. It is a love from which we are not (easily) released. Scripture repeatedly proves that God's love is inescapable. The steadfast love of the Lord never ceases. It is perpetually attached to us! We cannot get away from it. Even if we choose to ignore it, God's love follows us all the days of our lives. The Hebrews of the Old Testament call it the *hesed* of God. The Greeks of the New Testament call it the *agape* of God. Whatever you choose to call it, we Christians fundamentally believe that God *is* love, and this love is perfectly embodied in and demonstrated through Jesus Christ. And, even if we wanted to get away from it, God's commitment to us will not permit it. This love is unfathomable, unchangeable, unconditional—and it is fused to us! It is a love that will not let us go, despite our bad decisions or poor choices. It is a love that does not turn away, despite our antics or attitudes. It is a love that heals us and holds onto us. It is a love that encourages us and equips us, and empowers us. And that love—that God—is united to us.

In the midst of all our life's relationships, God's love illuminates our realities to prove to us that God is always on our side. As you read this book on God's benevolence, the sermons Johnson shares with us will grant us an opportunity to look at the myriad relationships that pepper the pages of our Bible and reveal to us how they mirror the relationships we each have known. Then, with the precision and practicality of a thoughtful pastor, he shows us how the bonded love of our God shines a light of care and compassion on all those created in God's image. And in what can best be received as a "pastoral plus," Johnson closes each message with a prayer for us to know the love of God in new and real, and palpable ways. These messages of God's love invite us to appreciate the anointed Man of God who has taken the time to carefully and courageously present God to us. But more importantly, this book should compel us to love the God of boundless, bonded love all the more. To <u>that,</u> God be all the glory!

Rev. Dr. Marcus D. Cosby
Senior Pastor
Wheeler Avenue Baptist Church
Houston, Texas

ACKNOWLEDGMENTS

I am blessed to have so many who have encouraged and inspired my writing of this book. I am grateful to Dr. Marcus D. Cosby who graciously consented to writing the foreword for "Bonded Love." His friendship of over 25 years, preaching, and writing have been an immeasurable benefit to me, and I am honored to have him commend this book.

I am indebted to the people of Metropolitan New Testament Mission Baptist Church of Albany, New York, where I am privileged to serve as pastor. I am grateful for their prayers and support as I worked on this project. More specifically, I want to express my deepest appreciation to the leaders and staff for their partnership in ministry that enabled me to give of myself to write.

I am thankful to Lois Coleman for her exceptional transcribing skills, Lisa DeJesus for her excellent skills in editing; Carlise Lovelady for editing and contributions to the prayers and content; Kim Brown for her assistance with printing, and a special word of thanks to Brittany Peoples for helping me get this project across the finish line.

To my wife, Angela, who is my best friend, my ministry partner, and my greatest source of encouragement. She has constantly prodded me to write, and I am so thankful to her. Ultimately, I give praise and glory to God.

I am thankful to the focus groups at Metropolitan, who gave great insight and contributions to the project.

Jesus - who is the lover of my soul - has encouraged me to share, speak, write, and witness about his bonded love. I John 4:19 sums it up: "We love Him, because He first loved us."

INTRODUCTION

Some years ago, I was preaching a spiritual enrichment week for Florida Memorial University in Miami, Florida, for my friend Dr. Wendell Paris, who, at the time, was the Dean of Chapel. A storm had come through the City of Miami the day before I was to arrive. When I got there, I saw damaged buildings, downed power lines, and palm trees that were bent over. I said to Wendell, "My goodness, this is horrible! A horrible tropical storm has come through! Your buildings are destroyed, and even the palm trees have been destroyed!" He said, "Oh no, Damone, not the palm trees. Our buildings have to be replaced, and the power lines have to be fixed, but our palm trees are fine." I pointed to one that was bent over, and I said, "Look at it. It's destroyed." He said, "No, it's bent over, but the thing about the palm tree is that its roots run so deep that it's down now, but as soon as the sun shines on it, it is going to rise again."

That is how God's love shines through our flawed relationships. Sometimes our relationships are bent over; sometimes, our relationships go through storms, and sometimes our relationships go through stress and strain. It appears that they are bent over; flawed; broken; damaged; never to be repaired. But when God's love shines on it, God's love is able to restore, renew, revive, and make it even better than it was before.

I experienced that in my life. I was born June 9, 1974, in Cook County Hospital to parents who were teenagers and in no position to take care of a baby. About six weeks later, they put me up for adoption. My adoptive parents, Delories J. Gross-Johnson and Paul Edward Johnson - who were looking to have children - decided to adopt. The adoption agency director shared something very interesting with my parents that as I began to grow, the doctors noticed my legs were not growing properly. They were somewhat deformed, flawed. They did not know if I was ever going to walk, and they said that if I ever did walk, I would have to have corrective braces for the rest of my life. They were not even sure if I would be able to walk at all. And my parents said, "We want to adopt him anyway." Of course, I was reared and raised in an extremely loving family with a wonderful, wonderful mother who raised me. My parents divorced when I was five, and my mother took the responsibility in rearing and raising me in the fear and admonition of the Lord. But God's love shined through. Even as a physically flawed baby, God's love still shined through on me.

I do not know if your relationships are physically flawed or spiritually flawed, financially, emotionally, or psychologically flawed, but I do want you to know God's love shines through. God's love can still strengthen, empower and equip you in any relationship you may have, whether it is husband and wife, parent and child, brother and sister, friends, a next, or an ex. God's love can shine through.

I was an assistant pastor of Ebenezer Baptist Church in Indianapolis, Indiana, for three and a half years under the pastorate of Dr. Thomas L. Brown, Sr. There was this one youth party where they turned off all the lights in the fellowship hall, and they gave out these little candles that everyone was supposed to shine. They were trying to emphasize Matthew 5:16 - *Let your light so shine before men, that they may see your good works and glorify your Father in heaven.* I could not get my light to shine, no matter what I did. So, I asked one of the teenagers for help, and she came over to me, took my candle, shook it, broke the top off, and said, "Reverend Damone, ain't nothing wrong with your light. You just have to shake it and break it to get it to shine."

Sometimes in life, life breaks us and shakes us, but God uses that to get us to shine for others, to illuminate a path of restoration for other people. My prayer is that as we look at these flawed relationships through the Bible, you will be able to see God's love shining through, not only the relationships in the biblical text but begin to shine through in your relationships. Keep shining!

Chapter 1

ALMOST DOESN'T COUNT
(Genesis 21:14-17)

Genesis Chapter 21:14-17 reads, "And Abraham rose up early in the morning, and took bread, and a bottle of water, and gave it unto Hagar putting it on her shoulder, and the child, and sent her away: and she departed and wandered in the wilderness of Beersheba. And the water was spent in the bottle, and she cast the child under one of the shrubs. And she went and sat her down over against him a good way off, as it were a bowshot: for she said, Let me not see the death of the child. And she sat over against him, and lift up her voice, and wept. And God heard the voice of the lad; and the angel of God called to Hagar out of the heaven, and said unto her; what aileth thee, Hagar? fear not; for God hath heard the voice of the lad where he is."

One of the things I love about the Word of God is that the Bible is very clear about showing us the good sides and the bad sides of people. Some people have great qualities, but some do not have the best qualities. The Bible is very clear and open about showing us different facets and different sides of people. I like that because I am not perfect, and, therefore, I cannot identify with somebody who is perfect. It is hard for us to identify with someone who has a perfect relationship, a perfect family, a perfect home, and a perfect life. That is not our reality. So, it is good to look at people who get it right but sometimes get it wrong and to show us that God's grace is able to shine through us even when we get it wrong.

That happened in our text in this young lady's life by the name of Hagar. Hagar was the servant of Sarah, who was the wife of the Patriarch Abraham. Abraham and Sarah go through different changes that result in Hagar going through some issues in her life. It all started with *Sarah's supplication*. God promised

Abraham that he was going to have a son and that the nations and the world would be blessed through his loins. The only problem is he is about 90 years old when he gets this promise. His wife is 80. They could not have children when they were younger. Sarah was barren, and now at 80 years old and her husband at 90 years old, God went to Abraham and said, I am going to bless your seed. In fact, the nations of the world are going be blessed by you. Look up at the stars, Abraham. That is how many descendants you are going to have. Look down at the grains of sand because that is how many descendants you are going to have. That was the promise, and the promise was so far-fetched that Sarah, when she heard it, laughed within herself, basically saying, I am old, and my husband is old. Will I really have such pleasure? The Lord asked Abraham why Sarah laughed. Did she doubt that she could have a child in her old age? Is there anything too hard for the Lord?

But do not get too mad at Sarah because some of us laugh at God's promises too. God has shown you and revealed some things to you, and it seems so far-fetched, so fanciful, that you are laughing at the promise of God.

That was the promise, and here was the problem. Abraham and Sarah were way past childbearing age. Then, of course, there was his condition. According to Romans 4, Paul says that Abraham's body was *dead*. At that time, there was no Viagra! So, you have a condition issue, a woman who was 80, and her husband who was 90. How was this going to happen? Since they could not figure it out, they came up with a plan themselves. It says in Genesis, Chapter 16, that Sarah prayed. She supplicated to her husband, Abraham. She said, look here, I've got a servant girl by the name of Hagar. You can just be with her, and she'll have a son, and since she's under me, it would sort of be like ours as well. That was the plan she came up with, and so they decided to go against God's plan. Just let me say this, whenever you get ahead of God and try to create your own plan and procedure and not follow his will and his way, trouble is getting ready to happen.

So, Abraham and Hagar had a son. Here is the interesting thing about Abraham, when Sarah suggested he connect with Hagar, he did not put up any resistance. He did not put up any debate or any argument. He said, okay, baby, if that's the way you want it, okay. Abraham and Hagar connected, and they had a child and named him Ishmael. The problem is Ishmael has some issues because whenever you step outside of God's plan, you will have some issues.

Then, God made good on his promise. Abraham was 100 years old; Sarah was 90; they had a son and named him Isaac. God said to name him Isaac, which means *laughter,* because Sarah laughed at the promises of God. She laughed at the promise of God, but God always gets the last laugh. God made good on His promise, and she said something. In Chapter 21, Verse 6 she said, *"The Lord has made me to laugh so that all around here can laugh with me."* What she was saying was this laughter was different from the laughter before. The first laughter was a laugh of disbelief. This laugh was a laugh of amazement and praise after she looked at what God had done. He did something miraculous in her life, and it made her laugh.

See, whenever God shows up in your life and does something that nobody thought could happen, not even yourself, it is going to make you laugh. Whenever your back is against the wall and God brings you out, it will make you laugh. Whenever God does things beyond time, when everybody thinks you are behind time, people will not understand it. God may not come when you want Him, but He is on time, every time, in time, and it makes you laugh!

Let me stop and ask you something, *Has God ever made you laugh? Has He ever done something so good in your life that you just find yourself laughing? Has God ever blessed you so good? Has God ever done something so well? Has God ever over-poured blessings on you so well that you could not even figure it out; you just had to laugh at it?* Yes, I am telling you God will make you laugh! God will do something so outrageous. He will do exceedingly, abundantly, above all you can ask or think. God will open windows of heaven, pour you out blessings you do not even have room enough to receive. God will make you laugh! God made good on his promise to Abraham. Isaac, the child of promise, was born. Imagine that! Abraham now had two sons. Now here is the situation; here is the family matter: It is now Abraham and his wife, his other son, and the baby mama. It is in the text. I did not make it up; this is in the text. This puts reality TV to shame! This puts the soap operas to shame! All of this is in the Bible! As they were going about their lives, I wonder what that was like? Abraham was looking at his miracle and his mistake. He was looking at his promise and his problem. He was looking at the child God promised him and the one he came up with.

As the boys grew, they had a party for Isaac, and at the party, Ishmael started mocking and making fun of Isaac. In fact, it is a little play on words because in the Hebrew language, Isaac means *laughter*. Ishmael was making fun of Isaac. He was *Isaacing* Isaac. He was laughing at laughter.

Sarah saw it happening, and she went to Abraham and told him *that boy and his momma have to go!* Now, Abraham was in a tough situation. His wife said she had to go. That was his son and his baby's momma, but he had to do it. *Genesis 21:14 (NLT) says, "Abraham got up the next morning, prepared food and a container of water, and strapped them on Hagar's shoulders. Then he sent her away with their son…"*

Now *Sarah's supplication* has moved to a *sorrowful situation*. First, it shows us a family that was broken because they were together at one time. That which was just together was now broken. Whenever you go against God's plan and start doing your own thing, it will show up in your family. Not only was the family broken, but there was some financial bondage. Genesis 21:15 said Hagar spent all she had. Now she did not have anything. She was just trying to make ends meet because when you go against God's plan, not only will it show up in your family, but it will also show up in your finances.

Hagar's future was bleak. She was wandering in the wilderness. She was wandering in Beersheba. Beersheba is a wilderness place. It is a dry place, and there she was wandering in the wilderness. She was living in a mansion, and then she was wandering in the wilderness. She was living in a great place - a high place of prosperity - but then she was in poverty as a consequence of going against God's plan, purpose, and program. Hagar was in a rough place. She was lost and lonely, and you can be lonely in a crowd. You can make $100,000 and still be lonely. You can live in a big house, have a great car, have an awesome career, and still be lonely. Because when you go against God's plan, it will show up in your future and make you lonely.

So, we move now from this *sorrowful situation* and from *Sarah's supplication* to the *son's separation*. First, this was a paternal separation. Ishmael was now separated from his father. Abraham had to put his son and his son's mother out. There was now a separation between father and son. Economically, they were separated. Abraham gave Hagar a flask of water and some bread, just enough to get Ishmael and his mama out of his face. I cannot help but ask some questions of Abraham. Abraham, why does a judge have to make you buy your child anything? It is your child, Abraham. Abraham, who was going to be the male role model for your child? All you gave him was a flask of water and some bread and said goodbye! Really Abraham? Really?

There was paternal separation, but then there was also maternal separation. In Verse 15, Hagar separated from Ishmael. Now, he is a teenager, and she is just a young, single mother trying to raise her son. There were two separations, but they were for different reasons. Don't miss this. Abraham chose to separate, but Hagar's separation was a consequence. She was trying to cope with what she was dealing with. She was just trying to make it. She was just trying to survive, and things had gotten so bad that she did not want to see her teenage boy die. She said she just needed a break. She could not deal with it psychologically and emotionally. She could not handle it in that moment, so she separated herself from her son. Understand that she was just trying to cope, and she said she did not want to see Ishmael die. She recognized that her situation had gotten so bad, she did not want to see her son go down the wrong path. She did not want to see him on drugs. She did not want to see him on alcohol, or all strung out. She did not want to see him hanging with the wrong crowd. She was trying to cope with this separation.

There was paternal separation and maternal separation, but thank God there was no eternal separation. Verse 17 says, *"And God heard the voice of the lad."* The father abandoned him, the mother separated, but God did not leave the boy. I want you to know something, someone reading this right now has had people you depended on abandon you. They have left you. I do not know if it is now; I do not know if it was when you were a child or when it was. But I want you to know something, God will not leave you, even if your parents have left you. I know because the psalmist says in Psalm 27, *"When my mother and my father forsake me, then the Lord will take me up."* When other people leave you, and other people abandon you, and other people forsake you, and other people desert you, how many of you know we serve a God who will never leave you, He will never forsake you, He will never abandon you.

Here is what I love about it. God heard the voice of the lad and where he was. He said I hear him where he is. In other words, right where he was, that's where God heard him. God will show up right where you are, right in your situation. And, in that *sorrowful situation*, God will show up right there. Why is this important? Because some people will say, why don't you come to church? Why don't you come on back to church? And the response would be as soon as I get myself together. Just as soon as I get right, I'm coming back. I promise you; I'll be back. But no, God will show up where you are. Not where you want to be, not where you wish you were, not where, if I had not made this choice, if I had not been with this person, if I had not married that person. No, He will show up right where you are in your messed up situation, in your messed up condition, as bad as you are, as messed up as you are, as wretched as you are, and as weak as you are! He will show up in your messed up condition, in your messed up situation with your family fractured, with your money messed up, with your relationship ruptured. How many of you know God will show up and hear you where you are, just like He heard the boy? I am so thankful for that because I have been in some bad places, but God showed up. I have been in some messed-up situations, but God showed up, and I am so glad He showed up. I am so happy He did not wait until I got right, but he heard me where I was.

Is there anybody thankful for a God that will meet you where you are? Is there anybody thankful for a God that will show up and meet you where you are? Somebody ought to praise Him because you have not always been in church, but right where you were, God showed up. For some of us, He showed up at the bar. For some of us, He showed up at the drug house. For some people, He showed up in prison. When He shows up, He will lift you to a whole other level. I am glad He came because I could not get to Him. How many know even though I could not get to Him, He came to me. He came to me right where I was! Is there anybody happy that He came where you were? Is there anybody glad that He showed up and came where you were? Bless His name! I came to let you know that God will show up where you are!

Some of us say, I almost lost my job. I almost lost my house. I almost lost my marriage. But, if God has left you anything in which you can survive and thrive, then almost doesn't count. Because the fact of the matter is like Hagar, we've been through some hard times. We've been through some rough times, but God has still kept us. You still have your job. You still have your house. You still have your health. You still have your family. You almost lost it, but God leaves you something to make it and not be destroyed. You have a reason to be thankful. Give God the praise and the glory! What counts is that God will show up for you and your loved ones. He shows up to let you know He is still with you.

For someone reading today, you are in a rough place. You are separated from friends, family, and familiar surroundings, but I want you to know that God has not left you; He is right there.

Let us pray:

Father, right now, in the name of Jesus, I thank you, and I honor you. Thank you, Lord, for being a God that will show up. Thank you, Lord for being a God that is so faithful, and so just, and so merciful and so kind, that even when other people abandon us, you will never leave us nor forsake us. Lord, I lift up those who have not accepted you as their Savior, but you have drawn them to you today. I lift up those who need to connect with your church, your family of faith. I pray for those who may have strayed away and been separated but need to come back and get reunited with you, God. I pray now that they would be obedient to the wooing and the leading of your precious Holy Spirit. I pray this now in the name of Jesus. We say hallelujah and amen.

Chapter 2

IT'S A THIN LINE BETWEEN
LOVE AND HATE
(2 Samuel 13)

In 2 Samuel 13:1, the latter part of Verse 1 says, *"and Amnon, the son of David loved her.* Verse 15 says, *"Then Amnon hated her exceedingly; so that the hatred wherewith he hated her was greater than the love wherewith he had loved her."*

How do you go from loving someone deeply and dearly to hating them with venom, hatred, and vitriol? How does it go from the person you could not wait to be in his or her presence to now you cannot stand being in his or her presence? How does that happen? How does it go from "Little House on the Prairie" to "A Nightmare on Elm Street?" How does that happen? How does a match made in Heaven turn into a marriage now marred by hell? How does that happen? How does one go from love to hate?

When I was a child growing up in Indianapolis, Indiana, on the 4th of July, we would go to what was called Conner Prairie where people would dress up as they did in the 1700s and 1800s. They would share with us the importance of Independence Day, the history of our nation, and the Revolutionary War. We learned all this historical and wonderful information. We loved watching the exciting fireworks show and display, I would notice the fireworks would go up very quickly, and then they would come down quickly. All that was left was some trash that other people had to pick up. That is what happens in relationships. They start with so much excitement, so much noise, and then after a while, they just fade out. So, it goes out just as quickly as it went up, and then someone must come behind and clean up the trash. How does that happen? I know there are different expressions, different experiences, and different events. I am not talking about what is going on with you; I am talking about what is going on in 2 Samuel 13.

Amnon was in love with this young lady named Tamar, and Tamar had position because she was a princess. She was the daughter of King David. Tamar was a pretty woman. The King James' version says she was "fair," but that description really did not do her justice. She was beautiful; she was gorgeous; she was pure. Tamar was a virgin, so she had her purity, and she was a practical woman because he said she could cook. So, she had position; she was pretty; she was pure, and she was practical, and Amnon started out in love with her. But 15 short verses later, he went from loving her to hating her.

I want to suggest that Amnon did not love Tamar in the first place. I know the Bible says he loved her, but I want to suggest that Amnon did not really love her to begin with, and here is why. First, he did not love her because the Bible says he was frustrated. Verse 2 says, *"And Amnon was so vexed."* The word vexed means to be distressed, to be in a tight jam, to be frustrated. Every time he saw her, she frustrated him. Love does not frustrate; love frees. John 3:16 says, *"For God so loved the world that He gave his only begotten son,"* and that did not frustrate us; it freed us. If every time you are around that person, you are frustrated, that is not love. I do not believe he loved her. He was frustrated, vexed, distressed, and upset every time she was around. That is not love.

Verse 2 also says, *"...he fell sick for his sister Tamar; for she was a virgin, and Amnon thought it hard for him to do anything to her."* What does he mean, do anything to her? He was thinking sex all the way. All he wanted to do was take her to bed. When you base the relationship on what you can get from them or what you can do to them, that is not real love. Love is not about what you can get from somebody. Love is about what you can give. How do I know that? Go back to what I just said, John 3:16 – *"For God so loved the world,"* watch this, *"...that He gave...."* Love is about giving, not about receiving.

When you enter a marriage, you cannot enter into it thinking it is 50-50. You must go into it thinking it is 100 and nothing because there may come the point when your spouse cannot give back to you as you give to him or her. That is why the marriage vows say, "in sickness and in health; for richer and for poorer." What if your spouse cannot work? What if he or she is sick and cannot give back to you? It would not be 50-50; it would be 100-0. You have to give everything. Even if you are the only one giving, knowing that you reap what you sow. That is what real love is about. Love is not about emotions; love is not about how you are feeling; love is not a feeling you thought you never felt before; that is not love, that is indigestion. The biblical concept of love is wanting the best for another person. That is what love is. Love is not about your emotion. It is not about what you feel. Love is an act of your will; it is about your volition. You have to make a decision to love someone. I decide to love you; I decide to assess your need and meet that need. When Jesus tells us to love our enemies, He is not saying to be emotionally attached to your enemies. Loving your enemies is an act of your will, not about how you feel.

Sometimes, couples come to me, telling me they just do not love their spouse. They just are not in love with him or her anymore. I would look at them and say, "You didn't think it was going to last, did you?" Then they would say, "What do you mean?" That warm, fuzzy love does not last. Love is about a commitment. Love is about a decision and, when you fall out of love, real love keeps you there until the feeling comes back. When you are not feeling it, and things are not going well, do not bail out. Stay there until it works itself out. Love is a decision of your will.

Amnon did not love Tamar. He said he loved her, but he did not love that girl; he was frustrated. The second reason I do not think he loved her is that he was fake. Verse 5 says, *"And Jonadab said unto him, lay thee down on thy bed, make thyself sick: and when thy father cometh to see thee, say unto him, I pray thee, let my sister Tamar come, and give me meat, and dress the meat in my sight, that I may see it, and eat it at her hand."*

Now here is what is going on, Amnon wants Tamar, but he is frustrated and does not know how to go about it. He has a friend (who was also his cousin), Jonadab, who was crafty, sneaky, conniving, and calculating. Jonadab says, what's wrong with you, man? Why are you so sick? Why are you going around so sad? You're the Prince. Your daddy is the King; He runs this place. Amnon explained what was going on. Jonadab said I've got something for that. All you have to do is act like you are sick, and when your dad comes to see you and asks you what is wrong, tell him you need Tamar to cook some food for you. When she cooks the food and brings it to you in your bedroom, then you can make that move."

Be careful about where you get your advice because the Bible says Jonadab was crafty. He was calculating, and he was sneaky. So, obviously, he was going to come up with a sly plan, but that does not mean it was the right plan.

Here is the issue with this plan. Amnon was operating in deceit and pretense. He could not be honest with Tamar. He had to develop a plan of deception to establish what he thought was love. You have to be open and honest about yourself. Amnon's identity, his name actually means "faithful." But he was acting phony. His name did not match his nature. Be careful when your name does not match your nature when your identity is not reality. That is true of us as believers in Christ. In 2 Chronicles 7:14, the Bible says, *"If my people which are called by my name…"*. Our name ought to match our nature. If we are true believers in Christ, it ought to affect our conduct and have an impact on our conversation. It ought to have an impact on how we live.

Amnon was not honest. He was fake and phony. He tried to pretend to be something he was not. Doesn't that happen in relationships? You claim you love your mate, but why can't you be honest with her if you love her? Why can't you tell her how you really feel if you love her? Amnon, why can't you be open and upfront with her if you love her? Why can't you tell her where you really work if you love her? Amnon, if you love her, why can't you tell her how many kids you really have? Amnon, if you love her, why can't you tell her where you are really going? If you love her, why can't you tell her where you really came from? Why can't you be upfront with her?

I am not suggesting you share everything on the first date saying things like, "you know, I've been in jail ten times. I have eight kids and five baby mamas. I've been strung out, but I've been sober for three months." I'm not saying to share any of that on the first date. You do not have to share it all at the beginning. If you do, there probably will be no second date. My point is about honesty and openness if you want your relationship to flourish and not fail.

Regarding the first couple, Adam and Eve, it says in Genesis 2:25, *"And they were both naked, the man and his wife, and were not ashamed."* It means Adam and Eve were open; they were exposed to each other, but they were not ashamed about it. I can be upfront. I can be open and honest with you, and there is no shame in that openness and in that honesty. We want to be open and honest with each other.

Brothers, have you ever had issues and could not be open and honest with women? That is a problem, and sisters, you should want openness because some brothers will wear a mask if you are not careful. Dr. Jeffrey A. Johnson, Senior Pastor of Eastern Star Church in Indianapolis, Indiana, tells a story about the San Jose Sharks, a hockey team. Like most sports teams, they have a routine they go through at the beginning of the game. They bring out the team, introduce the players - at least the starting lineup - they hype the crowd, and everybody gets excited. Then, they have a mascot who looks like a shark, and they usually bring him down from the ceiling on a rope. In one particular game, they introduced all the players as usual. They were skating around the rink, and they attempted to bring down the mascot, but for some reason, there was a malfunction with the rope, and he could only come halfway down. He was not down far enough to jump off onto the skating rink, so he was just suspended in the air. Since they could not take him all the way down, they drew him right back up. But there was an issue, to get the mascot back to the very top where he started, he had to go over a railing. They did not want to do that because they didn't ever want you to know who the person was in the mascot costume. But if the mascot was going to get over this railing, he had to take off the mask.

Sisters, before you allow a brother to get over a certain railing with you, you need to make sure his mask is off. Take some time to make sure someone's mask is off. And no matter how high you are, before they can get over some levels with you, they need to take off the mask.

But wait a minute. It is not just men who wear masks. Women can wear a mask too and be dishonest. So, men, you must also be careful and look under the woman's mask. You may wind up with something you did not expect. I'm in the Bible. In Genesis Chapter 29, Jacob is in love with a girl named Rachel, and he asks her father, Laban, for her. He said, well, if I'm going to give you my daughter, you have to work for me for seven years. Jacob fulfilled the seven years. So, on the night before the wedding, Jacob got drunk and went out with his buddies to party. Instead of putting Rachel under the veil, Laban put his oldest daughter, Leah, under the veil. Jacob was too drunk to realize it was not who he thought it was under the veil. This is in the Bible. Jacob consummated the relationship. He woke up the next morning, looked, and discovered it was not Rachel, whom he thought he married, but it was Leah whom he did not want. Brothers, make sure you stay sober. I know you want to have your fun, but make sure you stay clearheaded enough because you may wake up in the morning with someone else!

Amnon said he loved Tamar. I do not believe he loved her because he was frustrated. I do not believe he loved her because he was fake. Lastly, I do not believe he loved her because he acted a fool. 2 Samuel 13:12 reads, *"And she answered him, Nay, my brother, do not force me; for no such thing ought to be done in Israel: do not thou this folly.*" She continued in Verse 13, *"And I, whither shall I cause my shame to go? and as for thee, thou shalt be as one of the fools in Israel."* Now when a woman you are trying to get with calls you a fool, you are a fool! She said we cannot do this. First, because of who you are, you're the Prince. You're the King's son, and as the King's son, some things you should not do. Do you realize who you are? When you *know* who you are, there are some things you would not do. Amnon wanted Tamar. She appealed to his person. She started there with just who he was, his person. She said, wait a minute, let's be clear about who you are. You are the Prince, and the Prince shouldn't be involved in anything like this. We have to do this the right way. She said, let's go talk to the King, and he will give us permission, and we'll do this the right way, not the wrong way. Tamar tried to appeal to his personhood for him to truly understand who he was because when you know who you are, it ought to affect what you do.

It is the same concept for you and I. When you know who you are and whose you are, it impacts what you do. Well, who are you? According to the Bible, you are a chosen generation; you are a peculiar person, you are a royal priesthood, you are a holy nation. That is who you are. You are above and not beneath. You are the head and not the tail. The Bible says you are more than a conqueror. You need to know who you are. Own who you are. It impacts what you do, but it also impacts what you allow other people to do to you. You cannot lie to me. You cannot cheat on me. You cannot treat me like a dog. No, you will not call me that kind of name. I thought you knew! I thought you understood that I have self-esteem. You can let people know when they try to dog you out, look down on you, or are condescending; no, you will not treat me like that. You need to understand who I am. And, when they ask you what you are bringing to the table, let them know you are the table! I am bringing me and the table, and when I show up, it will be the best thing you have ever seen in your life! And, if you do not want me, it is your loss, not mine, because I know who I am!

Know who you are, and love who you are. Where does love start? Love starts with yourself. Jesus said, love your neighbor. How? As you love yourself. Start loving yourself, and when you love yourself, you are in a better position to love someone else.

Let us pray:

LORD, help us to walk in true love - a love that is unselfish, a love that seeks the good in others. Thank you so much for loving us with an unconditional love.
In Jesus' name. Amen.

Chapter 3

LET ME TELL YOU HOW THIS MAMA MADE IT
(I Kings 17:8-16)

1 Kings 17:8-16 says, "And the word of the LORD came unto him, saying, arise get thee to Zarephath which belongeth to Zidon and dwell there: behold, I have commanded a widow woman there to sustain thee. So he arose and went to Zarephath. And when he came to the gate of the city, behold, the widow woman was there gathering of sticks: and he called to her, and said, Fetch me, I pray thee, a little water in a vessel, that I may drink. And as she was going to fetch it, he called to her, and said, Bring me, I pray thee, a morsel of bread in thine hand. And she said, As the Lord thy God liveth, I have not a cake, but an handful of meal in a barrel, and a little oil in a cruse: and, behold, I am gathering two sticks, that I may go in and dress it for me and my son, that we may eat it, and die. And Elijah said unto her, Fear not; go and do as thou hast said: but make me thereof a little cake first, and bring it unto me, and after make for thee and for thy son. For thus saith the Lord God of Israel, The barrel of meal shall not waste, neither shall the cruse of oil fail, until the day that the Lord sendeth rain upon the earth. And she went and did according to the saying of Elijah: and she, and he, and her house, did eat many days. And the barrel of meal wasted not, neither did the cruse of oil fail, according to the word of the Lord, which he spake by Elijah".

Well, son, I'll tell you:
Life for me ain't been no crystal stair.
It's had tacks in it,
And splinters,
And boards torn up,
And places with no carpet on the floor – bare.

But all the time
I'se been a-climbin' on,
And reachin' landin's,
And turnin' corners,
And sometimes goin' in the dark
Where there ain't been no light.
So boy, don't you turn back.
Don't you set down on the steps
'Cause you finds it's kinder hard.
Don't you fall now--
For I'se still a goin', honey,
I'se still climbin',
And life for me ain't been no crystal stair.

The Harlem Renaissance poet Langston Hughes wrote this poem entitled "Mother to Son" to describe a message of a mama who had been through some struggle and some strain. In the poem, she encourages her son and tells him that life has not been easy; it ain't been no crystal stair.

I honor and thank God for mamas. Mamas rear and raise, love, encourage, and inspire us. Mamas are our best friends, and sometimes they are our only friends. I thank God for the mamas of our history. Mothers like Abigail Adams, who was a wife and a mother to United States presidents. Thank God for Elizabeth Cady Stanton, a leader in the women's suffrage movement. Thank God for a mother like Marie Curie, the mother of modern physics. Thank God for mothers like Sojourner Truth, who sojourned this nation and told the truth about slavery, and Rosa Parks, who was the mother of the Civil Rights Movement.

Thank God for a mother like Josephine Baker, who adopted some 13 children. Thank God for a mother like Kathy Hughes, a media mogul, and mothers like Tina Knowles and Beyoncé, who have built an entertainment legacy. Thank God for a mother like Michelle Obama, who is a leading woman, and a former first lady of the United States of America. We thank God for mothers like Sarah, the mother of Isaac, and mothers like Ruth, who was the grandmother of King David. Thank God for mothers like Rizpah, who protected her boys, and mothers like Salome, one of the last women at the cross and one of the first women at the tomb. Thank God for a mother like Elizabeth, who birthed John the Baptist, and thank God for Mary, who birthed our Lord and Savior Jesus Christ. We thank God for our mamas -- but motherhood is not always easy.

Being a mama gets hard at times, and what we find in I Kings 17 is a mama - a single mama - who had a man in her life but became a widow when her husband passed away. This mama was dealing with dead relationships and depleted resources in the most difficult time; a time of famine and drought, a time of chaos and crisis. But she made it. Let me tell you how this mama made it.

Elijah the prophet stood in front of the King of Israel, King Ahab, and told him it would not rain for three years. He said there would be a drought according to his word because God was sending a drought. Sometimes God sends droughts or difficulties in our lives to discipline us. He did that in Haggai 1:11. God sent a drought, a storm, and a problem to bring some discipline. If it is not discipline, then sometimes it is development. In Isaiah 58, God sent a drought not to discipline Israel, not to hurt or harm them, but to develop them. So, they began to fast and pray, and that drought led them to a closer relationship with God. If it is not for discipline or development, sometimes it is to change our direction, which was what was going on in I Kings 17.

God wanted to change Elijah's direction. As soon as he left King Ahab, God sent him to go and hide by the Brook Cherith. Cherith was a small brook that flowed into the Jordan River. By definition, it was a "cutting place, a separation" Elijah was there during a drought. It was not raining, very few people had food, and in Cherith - that cutting place – God sent ravens with food to feed him in the morning and evening. He was at a brook there right before Jordan. Elijah had his own Meals on Wheels, his own personal catering service in the middle of a drought, and he had a brook - his own spa - there to get refreshed and revived. It was a difficult place as it was a cutting place, but God provided for him. Things were going well for Elijah, even though there was a drought all around him. There can be trouble all around you, yet God can provide for you. It was going well, but God told him it was time to make a move - a shift in location. God told Elijah to get up, leave Cherith, and go to Zarephath. Wait a minute God. This is where I'm getting my provision. This is where I'm getting my refreshment. This is where I'm getting food. It was a good place, but there are times when God will show you that your present location is not your final destination.

There are times in life when God has to show you where He has you is good for right now, but it is just a temporary assignment. He wants to shift you to somewhere else, even if you are in a good place. You may have a certain job, and two years ago, you were just thankful for it, but you know it is a dead-end job. You know it is not going anywhere. But you are too afraid to make that next move to either start your own business or look for another opportunity. All because you do not realize that your present location is not necessarily your final destination.

Once I had to preach at the pastoral anniversary program at St. John Baptist Church - The Mighty Fortress - in Savannah, Georgia, for my best friend, Dr. George P. Lee III. I flew from Albany, New York, to Atlanta, Georgia, for my connecting flight to Savannah. Atlanta was not my final destination; it was just my connection. Atlanta is a huge airport, and if I was not careful, I could have gotten caught up and impressed by one of the largest airports in the world. I could have been so enamored with where I was, caught up in the restaurants and the bookstores, that I could have missed my connection and not made it to my final destination. That is where some of you are. You are so impressed with where you are, locally, that you are missing the connection that God wants to show you. Though good, though prosperous, though providing, your present location is not the final destination God has for you.

Elijah, get up from Cherith. I know it has been good, and it has been sweet, but this is not the final destination. I need you to go to Zarephath. It is a shift in location. It is a strange direction because it is the hometown of Queen Jezebel, the arch-enemy of Elijah. She was the woman who put a hit and threat on Elijah's life. That is where God told Elijah to go. He told Elijah to go to Zarephath, not go where Obadiah was. (Obadiah was the Governor of King Ahab's house.) In 1 Kings 18, Obadiah fed and took care of 100 preachers to hide them from Jezebel, but God said do not go there, go to Zarephath. It was a strange place. It was where Jezebel - the wicked, evil queen - was from.

Why would God send Elijah into enemy territory? He was trying to show him that He could provide for him and have victory even in enemy territory. Some of you cannot survive or make it if things are not going right, if things are not going smoothly, and if everyone around you is not a Christian. For some of you, you are the only Christian on your job, in your school, in your class, in your area, in your group, and you are trying to figure out why God? Maybe God wants to show you that He can give you victory and can use you in enemy territory. Everything will not be smooth, and everything will not be perfect. Every one there does not have to be a believer for you to have the victory still. You can have victory even in enemy territory. God can give you the victory in a strange place.

On Sunday, May 18, 2014, the Indiana Pacers and the Miami Heat played in the NBA playoffs. It was an exciting game because it was Game Six in Miami at the American Airlines Arena. The Indiana Pacers were down one game. The Miami Heat won three games, and the Indiana Pacers won two. If the Pacers had won Game Six, they would have forced a Game Seven. That is all they had to do. They had all-star players Paul George and Lance Stephenson. Still, they lost Game Six in Miami because they could not win in enemy territory. You must learn how to succeed even in enemy territory.

This shift in location for Elijah was a strange direction, but there was a strategic connection. God said there was a widow there that He had prepared to sustain Elijah. So, when Elijah saw this widow, this mama, this single mama, she was picking up sticks. This was a single mama who was working. Elijah told her to go and get him some water, and she did. Then he told her to go and bake him a cake. I can imagine her looking at him like, "You're a little demanding, aren't you, prophet?" But she said to him; I don't have a cake. All I have are some sticks, a cruse of oil, and a barrel with a handful of meal, and I plan to cook that for my boy and me, and we then we'll die. Now, Elijah, the prophet, told her to bring him a cake. She said she did not have a cake. She had sticks, oil, and some meal. When God gives you a command to do something, He will never give you the responsibility without also providing you the ability.

You may have to use some creativity to get it done, but He will give you everything you need to obey His command. The preacher said, bring me a cake. She said I don't have a cake. Alright, what do you have, Mama? I have sticks, I have oil, and I have meal. The woman did not have what Elijah asked for, but she did have the materials needed to give him what he asked for. She could fulfill his request if she used some ingenuity and creativity. Sometimes, the issue is not a lack of resources. The question is, are you willing to use some creativity and some ingenuity to do what God has told you to do? You do not have a cake, but you have sticks in your hand, oil and meal in your house, and knowledge in your head. If you get some desire in your heart, you can get it done. But you have to do what God is telling you to do and use some creativity.

Elijah said, bring me a cake. The woman had a choice to make because not only did he say bring me a cake, but he said he wanted her to bring him the cake first. This was during a famine and a drought. Nobody had food or rain. This was a national crisis.

You want me to give to you first, preacher? He said, yes, give me mine first. I want you to contribute to the work of God.

Here is the choice. The woman can take the cake and consume it with her son, or she can contribute it. If she consumes it, she already said she was going to die because that was her last food. Or she can contribute it and stand on the promise. She had a choice. When God asks us to contribute to His work, it is not a plan for death; it is a plan for life. When it is time to give to God your tithes, offerings, time, talent, or skills, it is never because God needs it. It is always a plan to sustain you. Now you have a choice. You can consume it and die, or you can contribute it and stand on the promise to live. It is your choice. But, do understand that when the man of God gives you a plan to give to the work of God, it is always a plan for life, never a plan for death.

Initially, it looked like God sent Elijah to Zarephath for this mama to sustain him, but God really sent Elijah there to help sustain the mama and her son. Elijah was already eating by the Brook Cherith; he did not need to go there to get a meal. He went there to be a blessing to this single mama. I am talking to a mama right now, and I am trying to help you understand how this mama made it. This mama made it because she took creativity, along with her ability, and put God first. Elijah said, make me a cake first. Notice the order. He said to make it and bring it first. Make it, then bring it. The problem with many of us is we make it, but we will not bring it. I know we make it because I have seen some cars you all drive, so I know you are making it. I know you make it because I know the jobs you all have with the government, the hospitals, and in education, so I know you make it. The question is not, do you make it? The question is, will you bring it, send it, or give it? It is not just enough to make it. He said to make it and bring it.

Now watch this. Elijah told the woman to make it and bring it to him first. This was a single mama and her son; they did not have anything. You want her to give you the cake first? Yes, put God's work first. He told her to make him a cake first. Put God first. Put God as a top priority, especially at this time in this COVID-19 pandemic crisis. You need God's provision more than any time in your life, and the way this mama made it in a national crisis was by putting God first. Wait a minute. Why first? Well, if there is a first, then there is a second. He did not say give me mine only; he said give me mine first, which means if you put God first, He will bless you to have a second, and then a third, and then a fourth, and then a fifth. The issue is not about supply; the issue is about priority. The Bible says in Matthew 6:33, *"But seek ye first the kingdom of God, and his righteousness; and all these things shall be added unto you."* God can provide for you and give you all these other things.

In 1 Kings 17:15, the Bible says the woman did it. She got the sticks, meal, and oil and put it together. She made Elijah a cake first, and the barrel of meal did not waste, nor did the cruse of oil fail according to the word of the Lord. The oil never went out of the cruse. The meal never went out of the barrel. Do not miss this. The oil and the meal were never full, but it was never empty. I have some money in my pocket. The pocket is not full of money, but it is not empty. I am just trying to show you that God has a way of sustaining you. Do you know what he did? He made her last, last. The cruse of oil, the meal, and the barrel was her last. And God made her last, last.

Some of you can testify that God can make your last, last. You know that refrigerator you need to replace, but you just do not have the money for it right now? You are surprised at how it is still working and still cooling your groceries. It is working because God will make your last, last. You know that car you have; I am talking about the kind of car you must pray before you drive, saying God, help me get from point A to point B. You putt-putt to point A and you putt-putt to point B. God made your last, last. You have that little job and are trying to figure out how you will make it when you have more month than you have money, and yet, someway God is still able to provide. You have food on your table; you have clothes on your back; you have everything you need. Do you know why? Because God is able to make your last, last. I thank God that He is a God that will provide everything that I need. Come on and give God praise because you know He will make your last, last. He will provide for you. Philippians 4:19 says, *"But my God shall supply all your need according to His riches in glory by Christ Jesus."* God will make your last, last. Do you want to know how this mama made it? She put God first, and when she put God first, God made her last, last.

Let us pray:

Father God, we honor you. We love you. Today, we thank you for the power and strength of your word. Thank you for teaching us your truths. Now, God, I pray for those mamas, particularly those single mamas trying to provide for their children. Lord, as she puts you first, I know God you will make her last, last. You are going to supply everything she needs. Thank you, Lord, for mamas who have sacrificed and served so that we could have what we needed, what we wanted, and what we had to have. God, my prayer today is for these mamas who are in need today, trying to figure out how to make it in this climate, in this crisis. God, provide what they need. Give them what they need, God. Give them whatever they stand in need of today, God. Your word says that if we put you first, your kingdom, then all these other things will be added. God, add to them what they stand in desperation for today. Thank you that you are a provider. Thank you that you are not short on your promise. You are able, God. I pray this in the matchless name of Jesus. Amen.

Chapter 4
THE BLESSED MAN
(Psalm 128)

"Blessed is every one that feareth the LORD; that walketh in his ways. For thou shalt eat the labour of thine hands: Happy shalt thou be, and it shall be well with thee. Thy wife shall be as a fruitful vine by the sides of thine house: Thy children like olive plants round about thy table. Behold, that thus shall the man be blessed that feareth the LORD. The LORD shall bless thee out of Zion: And thou shall see the good of Jerusalem all the days of thy life. Yea, thou shalt see thy children's children, and peace upon Israel."

Verse 1 says, *"Blessed is every one that feareth."* Verse 2 says "Happy," but it could be translated blessed. Then Verse 4 says, *"blessed that feareth the LORD."* Verse 5, *"The LORD shall bless thee out of Zion."* So, this chapter is all about the blessed man.

I am blessed, but not for the reasons you think. Some of us believe we are blessed because we have been able to move out of that apartment into our dream home. For others, blessed is when you no longer have just a GED but have gone from a GED to a master's degree. For some, blessed is when you no longer have to buy cubic zirconia but can get some real bling-bling! That is what some people think being blessed is.

But when the Bible talks about being blessed, one of the Hebrew words is *asher*. *Asher* is a blessing that comes from walking in the ways of God. You are blessed because you are not comfortable where you are, but striving to walk in the way, the will, and the word of God, even if it causes you to be uncomfortable. Even if it challenges you to come out of a place of comfort and convenience, you are willing to change and shift your life, so you are not only just receiving something from God, but you are literally transformed by the renewing of your mind. You have a state of mind and state of being, so now you can be transformed and really prove that which is the good, perfect will of the Lord. An acceptable will of God. That is *asher*. There is another word for blessed in the Hebrew language, *barack*, which literally means God has showered blessings on me - not just material things, but it means to be leveled. It means I am not up and down. Some people say sometimes they are up and sometimes they are down, but God wants you to be at a place where you are leveled. He wants you at a place where you are not up and down or flaky, but at a level place with peace that surpasses all understanding regardless of your circumstances. A place where you do not depend on people to make you happy. It means that you are at a place of blessing regardless of what people think, regardless of your predicament, and regardless of how you feel. Because you and I have a connection with God, that is why we are blessed. I am blessed whether you like me or not. I am blessed whether you accept me or not. I am blessed whether you want me or not. Why? Because my blessing does not come from the north, the east, the west, or the south. All my help comes from the LORD.

This Scripture talks about what it means to be blessed. I love the Book of Psalms. It runs a gambit of emotions. Psalms deal with real and genuine emotion because we have a real and genuine God. There are *Psalms of Lamentation*. For example, Psalm 142, *"I cried unto the LORD with my voice..."* Then, there are *Psalms of Thanksgiving*, like Psalm 107, *"O give thanks unto the LORD, for he is good..."* There are *Psalms of Confession*, like Psalm 51, *"Have mercy upon me, O God, according to thy lovingkindness: according unto the multitude of thy tender mercies blot out my transgressions."* Then, there are *Messianic Psalms*, which are psalms that speak prophetically about the Messiah, Jesus like Psalm 22, *"My God, my God, why has thou forsaken me?"* Then, there are *Psalms of Praise*, like Psalm 34, *"I will bless the LORD at all times and his praise shall continually be in my mouth."*

Then, there are *Psalms of Warfare*, like Psalm 35, *"Fight against them that fight against me."*

But the psalm we are covering now is called a *Psalm of Ascent*. It is a psalm that they would sing on their way to the temple. It is a temple psalm that they would sing as families were their way to Jerusalem. While they are on their way to the place of blessings, they would say, I'm blessed! Blessed! Blessed! God, I am blessed even before I get to my destination. I am blessed even before I get to my place. I do not have to wait until I get there to know that I am blessed. Sometimes you have to praise God not for achievement but for progress. I am not there yet, but I am still blessed. I finished one semester, and I am blessed. I have not gotten the job yet, but I got called for a second interview. I am still blessed. Some people did not get the second call to the second interview. You have to praise God on the way to the place of deliverance.

This writer talks about what a blessed man is like. He gives three things that make him blessed. In fact, you can envision this like a tree. The blessing takes root, it grows, and it bears fruit. It roots in a blessed faith. It grows by a blessed family and bears the fruit of a blessed future. These are the three things the man is blessed in – his faith, his family, and his future.

Going back to Psalm 128, Verse 1 says, *"Blessed is every one that feareth the LORD."* This is the blessed faith. Proverbs 9:10 says, *"The fear of the LORD is the beginning of wisdom."* To fear the LORD means you put God at the center of your life. Who is the most important person in your life? Is it God? God should be the most important person in your life. Not your job, not even your wife and your children, but God.

There was a time when astronomers thought the earth was the center of the universe, and they thought that everything revolved around the earth. It was what is called geocentric. Then Copernicus and Galileo came along and said no, the world is heliocentric, meaning the sun is the center of the universe, and the earth and all planets revolve around the sun. Funny thing, when they thought the earth was the center, all the calculations were off. But when they put the sun in the right place, everything else made sense. And so, it is with you, beloved. Your life may not seem to make any sense today. It could be that you do not have the SON in the right place. No, I am not talking about the s-u-n. I am talking about the S-O-N. The Son of God, Jesus Christ. When the S-O-N gets in the right place, everything else begins to make sense for you. A blessed man fears the LORD. He has the LORD at the center of his life, and he walks in His ways. Fearing the LORD is internal. Walking in His ways is external. When I have it right on the inside, then it shows up on the outside. When you fear the LORD on the inside, then it will make a difference in how you walk. What you think about God shows up in what you do, how you act, and what you say. You cannot separate it. If you do not fear the LORD and have it right on the inside, it will not show up on the outside.

Moving forward to the next passage, Verse 2 says, *"For thou shalt eat the labour of thine hands: Happy shalt thou be, and it shall be well with thee."* When God is at the center of your life, not your career, not your job, not your family, it shows up in your work, in your job, and in your productivity. The same verse in the *Message* translation of the Bible reads, *"All you that fear God, how blessed you are! How happily you walk on his smooth straight road. You worked hard and deserve all you've got coming."/* When you fear God, it is like a smooth road. You work hard, and blessings just start to come to you. It all happens when you put God first.

The writer says blessed is the one who fears the LORD, walks in His ways, he shall eat the labors of his hands. He is productive; that is the blessed faith. It starts with a blessed faith and grows into a blessed family. This man not only has blessed faith, but he also has a blessed family. Verse 3 says, *"Thy wife shall be as a fruitful vine by the sides of thine house."* Once you put God at the center, everything around you, my brother, gets blessed. In fact, your wife is blessed. He says your wife is *"as a fruitful vine."* Not just a vine, but a fruitful one. You may say to yourself, "My wife is not like a fruitful vine." Watch this, my brother. You have to cultivate a vine. She will not be fruitful if you do not cultivate her. You have to say kind words to her; be kind and spend some time with her if she is to be a fruitful vine. A fruitful vine speaks to productivity, being able to produce. We are able to produce in our lives because of who we are connected to. Jesus says it like this in John Chapter 15, *"I am the true vine. Ye are the branches."* Once I am connected to the vine that is Jesus Christ, I am able to produce. Jesus says that you are able to produce much fruit because you are connected to the source. Do not try to produce fruit if you are not connected to the right vine. If you are not connected to Jesus, it could be why your life is not productive.

In fact, let me ask you right now. My brother or my sister reading this, have you accepted Jesus Christ as your savior? Have you received Christ into your life? If not, I would like to extend an invitation. I want to give you a chance to be connected to the vine. Jesus said, *"Remain in me, as I also remain in you. No branch can bear fruit by itself; it must remain in the vine. Neither can you bear fruit unless you remain in me." (John 15:4 NIV.)* So it is that you cannot produce anything if you are not connected to Jesus Christ. Once you are connected, you do not have to make fruit happen. It happens automatically. In fact, you just become productive, just as Jamie Foxx said as he portrayed Ray Charles in the movie *Ray,* "I just make it do what it do, baby!" If someone gets jealous of you and your productivity, just tell them, I can't help it. I just make it do what it do! I am connected to Jesus, and Jesus blesses me. When his sap is running through my life, I am productive. All kinds of blessings just start happening because of whom I am connected to!"

You, too, can start producing fruit. I am talking about the Fruit of the Spirit: love, joy, peace, patience, gentleness, kindness, goodness, meekness, faith, and self-control. You start producing it because you are connected to the vine. If you are not experiencing that fruit, my brother, then you may be like the man in the Song of Solomon Chapter 7 whose wife was a fruitful palm tree, but the fruit was at the top. The man in Song of Solomon Chapter 7 says, I know my wife has fruit, but I am not experiencing that fruit. So, the man had to go to another level to get to the fruit. He started at the root. He was not experiencing any fruit there. So, he climbed to another place so he could experience the fruit. Maybe, my brother, you need to rise to another level to experience the fruit you want. And let me say this to you, my sister, do not ever lower your standards to give a brother your fruit. If your fruit is as sweet as you say it is, then believe me, a brother will climb the highest mountain; he will swim the longest river and tread through the deepest valley to get some of your sweet fruit. The reason why the man in the Song of Solomon could not get the fruit was because he had not gone to the next level. But once he did get to the next level, he was able to experience the fruit. It does not just stop with your wife; it extends to your children as well.

Continuing with Psalm 128, Verse 3, *"Thy children like olive plants round thy table."* Not only will you have a blessed wife, but your children will also be blessed. Blessed faith, blessed family, wife, and children.

Fathers, let me give you five things:

1) Fathers, you are needed. Even if your children are grown, you are needed. Your daughter is grown; you are needed. Your son is grown; you are needed. Even if they think they do not need you, you are needed. They need you. Your children may be parents themselves. They still need you.

2) You are accountable. You will have to give an account for how you raise(d) your children. Proverbs 22:6 says, *"Train up a child in the way he should go:*

And when he is old, he will not depart from it. " You are accountable.

3) You are irreplaceable. I know we live in a society that wants to marginalize men, but men, you are irreplaceable. There was this Hispanic family, and the father and son were on the outs. They had some disagreements and had not spoken in years. There was a lot of bitterness, anger, and hatred between them. But, the father had longed for a relationship with his son. So, he put an ad out in the newspaper. His son's name is Peco. The ad said, "Peco, this is your dad. I love you. I want to have a relationship with you. All is forgiven, Peco. Meet me at the courthouse on Sunday at 3 p.m." On that Sunday, 300 Pecos showed up. Three hundred sons named Peco showed up to have a relationship with their father. You are needed.

4) You need to sacrifice. Being an effective father speaks of sacrifice. You have to make some sacrifices. You have to sacrifice to take your children to the ballgame, to take them to certain things, or show up at school. You are going to have to sacrifice. You will have to cut off some things to sacrifice time with your children. I know some people say it is not about quantity; it is about quality. Well, if it is going to be of some quality, you need to spend some quantity. You need to spend some time with them.

5) *You will be rewarded.* God will reward you for being an effective father. A couple of years ago, I attended a funeral. The son gave a marvelous tribute to his father, who had passed. He said, "I'm a better man and am the father I am today because of my father." What an amazing tribute! Fathers, what would your children say about you when you are gone? When your grandchildren ask your children about you, what will they say about you?

You are blessed because you have a blessed faith, but you also have a blessed family. When he was in Australia leading the Allied forces, General Douglas MacArthur wrote this prayer that has become a poem called "Build Me a Son."

Build me a son, O Lord, who will be strong enough to know when he is weak and brave enough to face himself when he is afraid; one who will be proud and unbending in honest defeat, and humble and gentle in victory.

Build me a son, O God, whose wishes will not take the place of deeds; a son who will know Thee - and that to know himself as a foundation stone of knowledge.

Lead him, I pray, not in the path of ease and comfort, but under the stress and spur of difficulties and challenge. Here let him learn to stand up in the storm. Here let him learn compassion for those who fail.

Build me a son whose heart will be clear, whose goal will be high; a son who will master himself before he seeks to master other men; one who will reach into the future, yet not forget the past.

And after all these things are his, add, I pray, enough of a sense of humor, so that he may always be serious, yet never take himself too seriously.

Give him humility, so that he may always remember the simplicity of true greatness, the open mind of true wisdom, and the weakness of true strength.

Then I, his father will dare to whisper, "I have not lived in vain.

Fathers, pray for your children. The blessed man has a blessed faith, he has a blessed family, but then he also has a blessed future. I told you it roots in faith that grows by family, but it bears the fruit of a future. Look at Verse 5, *"The LORD shall bless thee out of Zion: and thou shalt see the good of Jerusalem all the days of thy life."* This speaks of a national blessing. The father now has gone outside of the house, and the blessing is seen in the whole nation. See, when you have a blessed faith that puts God first, it shows up, and you cultivate it in love by spending time and energy with your wife and rearing and training your children. Then they begin to bless the whole city and nation. What would happen if fathers would stand up, lead, love, and nurture their children in the ways of God? What would happen if they put God first and saw that God was at the center of their family? It will show up in the nation. In 2020, there were 15 shootings in two days in the City of Albany, New York. How would that change if fathers in Albany stood up? It shows up not just in your house but also in the community and in the neighborhood.

The Jewish people were very prideful about Jerusalem, their nation. They raised their children in a way that would give pride to the nation and the family. Parents, you ought to raise your children in a way that gives pride to the community and not just to the family.

Finally, the Scripture says in Verse 6, *"Yea, thou shalt see thy children's children, and peace upon Israel."* You are blessed, and not only are your children blessed, but your children's children are blessed. Proverbs 13:22 says, *"A good man leaves an inheritance to his children's children..."* Not just your children, but your children's children are blessed. Are you leaving an inheritance, a Godly inheritance? Yes, material and financial wealth are important, but so is a Godly inheritance for your children's children.

Carl Lewis, the great track star and Olympic gold medalist lost his father, William Lewis, in 1987. Carl Lewis loved his father so much. His father was his first track coach. Carl Lewis took the gold medal he won at the Olympics in 1984 and placed it in his father's casket. He buried the gold medal with him because he said, "Dad, you were my first coach, and I'm going to win another one." After he buried his father that August, he competed in the Olympics in Rome, Italy, and ran against Ben Johnson. Ben Johnson beat him in the hundred-yard dash. He looked up and said, "Dad, I tried to win it for you." Carl Lewis looked over at

Ben Johnson and waved. Ben pointed his finger at Carl in a manner that said, I got you, I got you! Carl just grabbed his stuff and went off. He said he saw something in Ben Johnson's eyes, but he did not say anything. He saw the way he was built. Everyone knows Carl Lewis was fast. He could have said, if anybody beats me, something is wrong. If anybody can outrun me, something is wrong. But he did not say anything. He just looked at Ben Johnson.

About six months later, they found out Ben Johnson had been taking steroids, so they took the gold medal away from Ben Johnson and gave it to Carl Lewis. Carl Lewis said, "Dad, I told you I was going to get another one for you, and I got one!" Because of the investment Carl Lewis' dad put in him, his dad got rewarded with a son that wanted to achieve something for him. When you make God the center of your faith and the center of your family, it blesses your future. You too can get a gold medal - not in the Olympics, not in track and field, but brother, you will get a gold medal in life. God wants you to be blessed.

Let us pray:

Father, right now, in the name of Jesus, I am thankful for you, God. I thank you for the fact that you bless us. I'm thankful that our blessings are true blessings, Godly blessings and not based on other people, other predicaments, other procedures, but based on our relationship with you. I pray right now for every father who is reading this. I lift up every father, and I pray that you would strengthen them. It's rough out there for fathers. It's rough out there for men. God, give us strength. Strengthen us, LORD, and help us to stay connected to you. So many of us are trying to be productive, but our connection has been cut off. I'm praying for every man reading this book who has a connection with you, oh God, because you are the true vine who establishes that connection. Establish it through prayer and Scripture. Establish it through walking with character and integrity.

I'm praying for those brothers who have lost that connection with you, those who are lost, God. You used to be important to them, but you are not as important anymore. God, I'm praying that they would use today as a day to reconnect with you, to connect with a son or a daughter, or to connect with a wife. But, before they connect with all of them, God, they need to connect with you. Why? Because you are the true vine. You are the one that is able to help us bear much fruit.

Thank you, LORD, for every man reading this right now. I pray for his family. I pray for his finances. God, I pray you keep us physically strong during this awful COVID-19 pandemic. I pray for his health. I pray you keep him physically strong. I pray for his finances and the 13 percent who are unemployed, God. I pray you keep the men reading these words financially secure and that you would supply every need they have. I know you can do it, LORD, and I thank you for it now in the name of Jesus. Thank you for men who will stand up in their families, in their communities, and in the power you have given them to be fruitful and productive for you, oh God. While the world, while society and criminal justice systems are coming against them, help them to stand and be productive despite the pandemic, to be productive in spite of a policy or a system that's against them. Help them to do it right now in the name of Jesus, and we seal this prayer with praise and thanksgiving. We just praise you right now. We adore you right now. In Jesus' name, Amen.

Chapter 5

BEFORE WE SEPARATE, LET'S COMMUNICATE
(Song of Solomon 1:7-12, 5:10-16)

Comedian and actor Kenan Thompson and his wife, Christina, separated in 2022 after 11 years of marriage and two children. Singer Miley Cyrus and her husband Liam Hemsworth, together ten years, divorced in 2021. Her parents, Billy Ray and Tish, filed for divorce after 30 years of marriage and five children, citing "irreconcilable differences." These separations happened between celebrities who have popularity, money, and position.

Someone is reading this right now on the verge of separation. Before you say, Pastor, that's not me. I'm not looking to separate. Remember, there can be all types of other separations before there is a physical and a legal one. It is more than just a legal divorce and a legal separation. There could be an emotional, psychological, spiritual, or sexual separation. There are all types of separations that come long before it gets to the court. In fact, those separations are what lead to the legal separations, so I want to encourage somebody that before you separate, try to communicate.

Marriage is kind of like a car. You must get the oil changed, do other maintenance, and get your tires rotated. All of that makes your vehicle run smoothly. In a marriage, there are specific checkups you need to help ensure your marriage is running smoothly, and one of the main things is communication. In fact, we give surveys to couples here in our Marriage Ministry at Metropolitan Church, and the most consistent issue that has often come up through the years has been communication. It may be someone not being heard or someone not being listened to, but it is the whole issue of communication. If you want to resolve communication issues, someone needs to open up and talk first. If you can resolve the communication issues, you will resolve about 80 percent of your other problems. It all starts with communication.

The Bible talks about how important that is. Proverbs 18:21 says, *"Death and life are in the power of the tongue."* Let us put that in the context of marriage. The death and life of your marriage are in the power of the tongue. Then, in I Peter 3:10, it says something interesting, *"For he that will love life, And see good days, Let him refrain his tongue from evil, And his lips that they speak no guile."* Let us put that in the frame of marriage. For he that will love life and have a consistently good marriage and see good days in his marriage let him refrain his tongue from evil and his lips that they will speak no guile. Communication is so vitally important.

I want to look at the Song of Solomon and see how this couple - Solomon, who is called the lover, and the Shulamite woman communicate and how their communication led to a wonderful, blissful relationship. Song of Solomon 1:1 says, *"The songs of songs, which is Solomon's."* The Song of Solomon is in the portion of Scripture called "Wisdom Literature."

The Old Testament is divided into three parts. The first part is the "Historical," which is the first 17 books; the second part is the "Poetical," which is the next five books; and the last part is the "Prophetical," which is the last 17 books. These five wisdom books are in the Poetical section: Job, Psalms, Proverbs, Song of Solomon, and Ecclesiastes. Solomon wrote the last three. Solomon wrote Proverbs when he was a middle-aged man. He wrote Song of Solomon when he was a young man and wrote Ecclesiastes when he was an older man looking back over his life. In Song of Solomon, we find a beautiful relationship. We get a chance to eavesdrop on the conversation between Solomon and his wife, the Shulamite woman. What I want you to notice first is that their communication was plentiful. Sixty percent of the Song of Solomon is Solomon and his wife talking.

Let me give you five reasons why you need to talk to each other:

1) If you do not talk, you will drift apart. You either communicate, or you disintegrate. It is not optional. You will drift apart.

2) Problems do not disappear just because you do not talk about them. Sometimes, we do not talk about issues. It is not just in marriage; it is in any context or any relationship, and we think if we do not talk about it, it will just go away. It does not go away because you do not talk about it. I tell married couples all the time in premarital counseling to deal with the issues now and get them on the table now, and here is why. There is nothing magical about the wedding date. Whatever the issue is today, after you say I do, it will still be an issue if you do not deal with it. So, the issues do not stop, change, or go away just because you avoid them.

3) Talking gives touching more meaning. Many of us want to get past the talking and just go to the touching. We will see in a while that there was some touching going on with Solomon and his wife. They got to the touching, but there was some talking before there was some touching.

4) Resentment will build up and fester if you do not talk. When you do not talk about issues, you just avoid them for whatever reason because it is a difficult conversation. You must be willing to have that courageous conversation.

5) Relationships are about deposits and withdrawals. If you try to make withdrawals and have not made deposits, it will not be good. One of those deposits is communication. Now I will admit, communication is different, particularly for men. We are just wired differently, so we communicate differently. In 2020 and 2021, our church could not have a summer youth camp due to the COVID-19 pandemic. Normally, you can walk around with the

little children during camp, even in our nursery, and observe how they communicate differently. The girls would be over in a corner, and they would be talking and giggling about their hair and different stuff. That is how they communicate. The boys would be in another corner with their trucks and cars going vroom, vroom, vroom, vroom, beep, beep, beep, vroom, vroom. That is how they communicate. It is a totally different communication.

Research shows women speak an average of 25,000 words per day. Men speak an average of 12,000 words per day. So, sisters, when you get home, you have used up about 15,000 of your words; you have 10,000 more to go. When your husband gets home, he has used up 11,999 of his words, so when you ask him how his day was, he only has one more word left, and he says, "Fine." He has used up his words, and you have 10,000 more to go. That is why it is so difficult.

Brothers, Ephesians 5:22 says, *"Wives submit yourselves unto your own husbands..."* and in Verse 25, it says, *"Husbands, love your wives, even as Christ also loved the church..."* When you love your wife as Christ loved the church, you are willing to sacrifice even though it may be difficult. Even though you may not talk as much and you may be faced with an issue that is difficult to talk about, because you love her as Christ loved the church, you should be willing to sacrifice. One of those sacrifices is having courageous conversations. It is not an easy conversation, but it is a courageous one.

Not only was it plentiful, but the communication was also positive. Song of Solomon 1:7 says, *"Tell me, O thou whom my soul loveth, Where thou feedest, where thou makest thy flock to rest at noon: For why should I be as one that turneth aside By the flocks of thy companions?"* Verse 8 says, *"If thou know not, O thou fairest among women..."* This is what Solomon said to her. This is what the husband said to the wife. *"O thou fairest among women, Go thy way forth by the footsteps of the flock, And feed thy kids Beside the shepherds' tents."*

If you go over to Chapter 5 in Verses 1-2, you will see how Solomon was talking to his wife. He was really rapping to his queen! He said, *"I am come into my garden, my sister, my spouse..." I sleep, but my heart waketh: It is the voice of my beloved that knocketh, saying, Open to me, my sister, my love, My dove..."* See, he was rapping. He said my love, and then he said my dove. You did not know that was in the Bible, did you?

Go back to Chapter 1. Notice what he said in Verse 8, *"If thou know not, O thou fairest among women, Go thy way forth by the footsteps of the flock, And feed thy kids Beside the shepherds' tents."* Now watch how he described his woman in Verse 9, *"I have compared thee, O my love, To a company of horses in Pharaoh's chariots."* Those were of high value. Then he said in Verse 10-11, *"Thy cheeks are comely with rows of jewels, Thy neck with chains of gold. We will make thee borders of gold With studs of silver.* Solomon was describing his wife and complimenting her. He started with her cheeks; then he went to her neck. Notice what he was doing. He started at the top, and, if you keep reading, he went to go to the bottom, but he stopped at the top because what was most important was not just the bottom, but how a woman thinks with her head. Amen!

That is what Solomon said about his wife. He was in love with her. Now let us look at what the wife, the Shulamite woman, said about Solomon in Chapter 5, starting at Verse 10, *"My beloved is white and ruddy, The chiefest among ten thousand."* She told him he was the best among 10,000! His head is as the most fine gold, His locks [now she's talking about his hair] are bushy and black as a raven. His eyes are as the eyes of doves by the rivers of waters, [she can rap too] washed with milk, and fitly set. His cheeks are as a bed of spices, as sweet flowers: his lips like lilies, dropping sweet smelling myrrh. His hands are as gold rings set with the beryl. His belly is as bright ivory overlaid with sapphire. His legs are as pillars of marble, set upon sockets of fine gold: his countenance [That means just how he is all over] is as Lebanon, excellent as the cedars. His mouth is most sweet: yea, he is altogether lovely. This is my beloved, and this is my friend, O daughters of Jerusalem. She said, *"O daughters of Jerusalem"* to let all her friends know this was the kind of man she had.

This is what it is about. It is about complimenting each other. It is about admiring each other. It is about showing affection toward each other and being positive toward each other. When was the last time you complimented your husband? When was the last time you complimented your wife? This is important because someone else might be complimenting them. So, if you are not complimenting her, who is? If you are not complimenting him, who is telling him how good he looks?

You may be saying, Pastor, that's just not me. I'm having trouble with that. Colossians 4:6 says, *"Let your speech be alway with grace, seasoned with salt, that ye may know how ye ought to answer every man"* [or woman]. Just let your speech be with grace. What is grace? Grace is when we have something we do not deserve. You may not even think your spouse deserves it, but it is about grace. Am I supposed to do all that for him? Yes. It is about grace, and grace does not give you what you deserve. Grace gives you what you do not deserve. So, apply some grace. Give them the grace to compliment them. The Scripture says, seasoned with salt. What does salt do? Salt adds some flavor. So, flavor your words - your communication - with some compliments; something nice. I know you think you can flavor it with arguing and debating, but flavor it with some grace.

Try this exercise. Every day this week, find one compliment you can give your husband or wife; just one. Try it for a week starting today. Find something nice to say. Maybe he took the trash out. Say, thank you. You did a good job. I have never seen anybody take the trash out as you do!" Whatever it is, just try something. You must season it with salt and grace. "Oh baby, you know you washed those dishes!" "Lord have mercy, look at you, oh my goodness, I love those shoes!" Season it with salt.

I want to pray for married couples right now. I want you to be praying for your spouse. This is one thing you can do if you are having trouble communicating. Start praying for them; start going to God for them.

Let us pray:

Father, right now in the name of Jesus, you called us to gentleness, to grace, and to kindness, God, and I lift to you wives who are reading this. I pray, God, that you are granting the grace to be sympathetic and to be compassionate, to be humble because you have transformed them through your Holy Spirit to be gracious women, women of honor, virtuous women, who are kind to their husbands, whose purpose is to walk wisely, that they may build houses of riches and inheritance.

So, Father, in the name of Jesus, I lift the wives to you, and then I lift up husbands. God, we are thankful for husbands who are watching your partners and are leaders in the home. My prayer, God, is that they would write your word in their hearts, and that you would place a hedge of protection around them. Lord, I thank you for the favor that rests upon every husband that is reading this today. They have found a wife, and your word says, "Whoso findeth a wife, findeth a good thing and obtaineth favor of the Lord." Now God, allow them to cherish their wives, walk in favor, and love you have for them. In the name of Jesus, I thank you, Lord for moving. Thank you for your strength. Thank you for your power. Thank you for your provision. Thank you for being a way maker. Thank you, Lord, that you are going to continue to bind families, bind marriages together with cords that cannot be broken, that you will bind them together in love.

Chapter 6

I'M IN THE FAMILY TOO
(Matthew 1:1-17)

"This is the genealogy of Jesus the Messiah the son of David, the son of Abraham: Abraham was the father of Isaac, Isaac the father of Jacob, Jacob the father of Judah and his brothers, Judah the father of Perez and Zerah, whose mama was Tamar, Perez the father of Hezron, Hezron the father of Ram, Ram the father of Amminadab, Amminadab the father of Nahshon, Nahshon the father of Salmon, Salmon the father of Boaz, whose mother was Rahab, Boaz the father of Obed, whose mother was Ruth, Obed the father of Jesse, and Jesse the father of King David. David was the father of Solomon, whose mother had been Uriah's wife, Solomon the father of Rehoboam, Rehoboam the father of Abijah, Abijah the father of Asa, Asa the father of Jehoshaphat, Jehoshaphat the father of Jehoram, Jehoram the father of Uzziah, Uzziah the father of Jotham, Jotham the father of Ahaz, Ahaz the father of Hezekiah, Hezekiah the father of Manasseh, Manasseh the father of Amon, Amon the father of Josiah, and Josiah the father of Jeconiah[c] and his brothers at the time of the exile to Babylon. After the exile to Babylon: Jeconiah was the father of Shealtiel, Shealtiel the father of Zerubbabel, Zerubbabel the father of Abihud, Abihud the father of Eliakim, Eliakim the father of Azor, Azor the father of Zadok, Zadok the father of Akim, Akim the father of Elihud, Elihud the father of Eleazar, Eleazar the father of Matthan, Matthan the father of Jacob, and Jacob the father of Joseph, the husband of Mary, and Mary was the mother of Jesus who is called the Messiah. Thus there were fourteen generations in all from Abraham to David, fourteen from David to the exile to Babylon, and fourteen from the exile to the Messiah."

"All in the Family" is a sitcom that first aired in the 1970s about a working-class white family living in Queens, New York. The family's patriarch is Archie Bunker (Carroll O'Connor.) He is an outspoken, narrow-minded man, seemingly prejudiced against everyone who is not like him or his idea of how people should be. Archie's wife, Edith (Jean Stapleton), is sweet and understanding, though somewhat naïve and uneducated. Her husband sometimes disparagingly calls her dingbat.

Three spinoffs came from the sitcom: *Maude*, *Good Times*, and *The Jeffersons* - my favorite. You know that familiar song:

"We're movin on up, to the East Side
to that deluxe apartment in the sky.
Movin' on up to the East Side.
We finally got a piece of the pie.
Fish don't fry in the kitchen.
Beans don't burn on the grill.
Took a whole lot of trying just to get up that hill.
Now we're up in the big leagues
getting our turn at bat.
As long as we live, it's you and me baby.
And there ain't nothing wrong with that.
We're moving on up, to the east side.
We finally got a piece of the pie."

Spiritually, we are spinoffs of the family of Christ - grafted in because of the redemptive, completed work of Christ on Calvary. In biblical times, family genealogies were important. They determined what status one had in society. It had much more importance than what we place on it today. After the Exile, when the Israelites returned to Jerusalem, those who were priests had to prove their ancestry in order to return to the priesthood.

For people unable to prove their genealogy, it was almost like being an American in a foreign country who does not have their passport or someone who needs to show proof of vaccination but does not have their card. I want to look at this genealogy carefully and prayerfully and see how we are spin-offs who declare, "I'm in the family too."

I'm in the family, too because God implements uncommon promises to achieve His purpose. Matthew 1:1 reads, *"The book of the generation of Jesus Christ the son of David, son of Abraham."* The word *genealogy* has as its root word *genesis*. It could read *from the beginning* or *from the genesis* of Jesus Christ. Like a bridge over a great span of water, Matthew connects the Old Testament and the New Testament with Jesus' genealogy. Luke gives the genealogy as well. Not in Chapter 1 of his gospel but in Chapter 3 at the baptism of Jesus, when the voice of God comes out saying, *"This is my beloved son, in whom I am well pleased."* Luke goes back not 42 but 77 generations. All the way back to Adam to show that in the first Adam, the human race was created. Out of the second Adam, Jesus, a new race was created. As it says in 2 Corinthians 5:17 (NKJV), *"Therefore, if anyone is in Christ, he is a new creation; old things have passed away, behold, all things have become new."*

God made a promise to David in 2 Samuel 7:13-14. God promised David, *"He shall build an house for my name, and I will stablish the throne of his kingdom for ever. I will be his father, and he shall be my son."* It was a *purposeful promise*. He will build my temple. It was a *perpetual promise* because he said his throne would last forever. It was a *parental promise* he said, he will be my son, and I will be his father in a very unique way.
It did not happen immediately. There was a division of the kingdom. First was the Exile, then the Return, and after that, the Inter-testament era. Then Jesus showed up as the son of David. It shows us that God's promises take some time. They are not always immediate, but they are certain.

What about Abraham? God told Abram from his seed; the nations would bless one another. It took 42 generations. Then in Galatians Chapter 3, Paul said, *"Now to Abraham and his seed were the promises made. He saith not, And to seeds, as of many;*

but as of one, And to thy seed, which is Christ. And this I say, that the covenant, that was confirmed before of God in Christ..." It didn't look like it at first. Abraham only had a plot of land to bury his wife. He never saw the land. His descendants were enslaved. They were freed and then came the Civil War. Other nations defeated Israel, a nation which is about the size of the State of Vermont. It did not look like the promise was going to happen. Forty-two generations later came the seed, Jesus Christ, the seed of Abraham. God's promises take time.

God does not move when we want Him to. You may wish God would move faster. You wish His promises would come quicker. God has to teach us patience. James 1:3-4 says *"...the trying of your faith worketh patience. But let patience have her perfect work, that ye may be perfect and entire, wanting nothing."* Some of you have been waiting on God to do something in your life. Some of you have been waiting on God to do something in your family and in your finances. You are wondering how long it will take? I'll tell you, *"...they that wait upon the LORD shall renew their strength; they shall mount up with wings as eagles; they shall run, and not be weary; and they shall walk and not faint." (Isaiah 40:31.)*

Sometimes you are waiting on the promise, and the situation seems to be getting worse, not better. That happened with Abraham and David. Their sons were disappointments. David's son Solomon, the wisest man to ever live, started with great potential but intermarried foreign women who turned his heart away from God. At the end of his life, he said, "...vanity of vanities; all is vanity," meaning everything is meaningless. What about Abraham's son? Isaac is presented as a weak, puny man. When life disappoints you, keep trusting God.

Maybe God is taking His time because He has a major blessing for you. In Genesis, God said let there be light, and it happened immediately. Why did it take Christ Jesus 42 generations to come? Why did he not come immediately? Because God was building a temple, it took some time. If a person wants to build a slipshod house, it can be built in a few days. But when a person wants to build a temple, it can take years. God was building a temple. God is not trying to give you just any kind of blessing. God is trying to provide you with a tailor-made, big, awesome blessing that is going to blow your mind!

God is not overly concerned about the product. He is concerned about the process. It is not just deliverance, but it is development. When God delivered the children of Israel from Egypt, it took them 40 years to get to the promised land. They could have made the trip in 11 days. Forty years in the wilderness was development. God was concerned about their process. He is concerned about your development. God does not just want to give you a gift; God wants you to grow. In order to grow, He has to take some time. The question for many of us is not if the blessing is ready for you, but rather, are you ready for the blessing? Are you mature enough to receive what God wants for you?

I'm in the family too, because God includes unlikely people to be a part of his pedigree. Matthew 1:2-16 goes through a long list of begets. The list shows some unlikely people that are part of the family of Jesus. Notice the five women in the Genealogy of Jesus the Messiah. That is unusual because ancient genealogies did not mention women. Matthew names five women. Matthew 1:3 mentions Tamar (Judah's daughter-in-law.) In Verse 4, Rahab is named. In Verse 5, Ruth is mentioned. Then in Verse 6, the mother of Solomon, the wife of Uriah is listed - as if Matthew cannot bring himself to say the name Bathsheba. Verse 16 speaks of Mary, the mother of Jesus. Each of these women were surrounded by scandal. Tamar's story in Genesis Chapter 38 was filled with scandal. It was filled with betrayal, prostitution, and deception, but there she is in the ancestry of Jesus.

What about Rahab? The rabbis said there were only four women of unusual beauty in Israel's history: Sarah, Rahab, Abigail, and Esther. The rabbi also said that when the church of Israel left Egypt in the Exodus, Rahab was ten years old. For the following 40 years of their wandering, she prostituted herself until the conquest of her city. She is part of the redemptive purposes of God.

Ruth the Moabitess was the granddaughter of Eglon, the King of Moab. If you look at the history of Ammonites and the Moabites, their history was filled with incest and other unmentionable acts. In the Book of Deuteronomy, God commanded that they should not come to His house even to the 10th generation.

What about Mary? In John Chapter 8, the Pharisees, who did not like Jesus, said in a dialogue with Jesus, Abraham is our father. They were throwing shade, bringing up some backstreet gossip about the paternity of Jesus. They were saying, in essence, we know who our father is. Who's your daddy?

What about the men? Abraham lied about his wife and told the King of Egypt that she was his sister to save his own neck. David took a man's wife then took that man's life. They are in the family tree of Jesus. If they can get in, I can get in, and you can get in the family. We have some rough reputations. We have some Abraham-like attributes and some Davidic demons. We have some Ruth and Rahab ways and some Tamar tendencies. No matter your reputation or the mistakes you have made, and no matter your failures, even with your messed up reputation, you can come on in the family.

I'm in the family too, regardless of reputation and regardless of race. Four of the five women mentioned were not Jews. Tamar, Rahab, Ruth, and Bathsheba were Gentiles. The text is tailored to teach us that you can get in the family regardless of your race. Jesus is the King of Kings and the LORD of Lords of all people.

The great Dr. E.V. Hill was asked, Was Jesus a Caucasian as depicted in the paintings? To which he replied, "I don't know anything about a white Jesus. I know about Christ our Savior who was named Jesus. I don't know what color He is. He was born in the brown Middle East, He was smuggled into black Africa, He was in heaven before the gospel reached white Europe. I don't know what color He is. I do know one thing. If you bow at the altar with color on your mind, you'll get up with color on your mind. Go back again and keep going back until you no longer look at His color but His greatness and His power. His power to save."

I'm in the family too, regardless of reputation, regardless of race, but also regardless of rank. Aram is named in Matthew 1:3. He was the father of Aminadab. Aminadab was enslaved. He was in servitude with his hands tied and fettered. He was in the Genealogy of Jesus who would come and set the captives free.

In Verse 7, Abia fathered Asa, which some interpret as Asaph. Asaph, the musician of the Old Testament, in the genealogy of the One who has more songs written about Him than any other person. Zorobabel is named in Verse 12. He is known as the one who led the rebuilding of the Temple after the exile. He is the one who encouraged the people to build up again out of the desolation. He is in the very ancestry of the One who would later come and cleanse that Temple and would say, *"Destroy this temple and in three days I will raise it up." (John 2:19)*. Verse 13 talks about Abiud, Eliakim, and Azor. They were prophets who were in the ancestry of the One whom the prophets spoke. Verse 14 records the names Sadoc and Achim. Both were priests in the ancestry of the Great High Priest. Your race, rank, nor reputation can keep you from being in the family of God. All of us can be in the family because we all need to be redeemed.

Finally, I'm in the family too because God involves himself in unfolding periods to accomplish his plan. Verse 17 says, *"So all the generations from Abraham to David are fourteen generations; and from David until the carrying away into Babylon are fourteen generations; and from the carrying away into Babylon unto Christ are fourteen generations."*

In the Bible, the number seven is the number of completion and perfection. The number seven and its multiples are important in the Biblical record. God created the world in six days. On the seventh day, He rested. In the book of Daniel, there are seven visions. The nation of Israel was in exile for seventy years. In the Book of Revelation, there are seven churches of Asia minor, seven golden candlesticks, seven bowls, seven seals, and seven trumpets. It is not by accident that Matthew uses three sets of 14 to explain the family tree of Jesus Christ. It shows that God is sovereign over all history. God has complete control. It is good to know that God is in charge in the midst of the Covid-19 pandemic and increasing financial crises.

All three sets of 14 generations started out with great potential but ended in failure. First, Abraham was the father of the faithful, but he failed when he lied about his wife. Then he was not prepared to wait on God's promise and had Ishmael with Hagar. Second, David's royal lineage had great promise, but then there was the failure of royalty. The third was the failure of exile. Each of these generations started with great promise and ended in failure.

Their failures show the faithfulness of God. They had to fail in order for us to have Jesus. There would have been no need for Jesus if there was no failure. No matter what your failure is, it will not stop God's faithfulness. I suggest God allows some failure in our lives so He can show you His faithfulness. God is faithful! God is faithful! God is faithful!

"Great is thy faithfulness. Great is thy faithfulness. Morning by morning, new mercies, I see. All I have needed thy hand has provided. Great is that faithfulness, Lord unto me."

Let us pray:

Lord, thank you for being a faithful God. Thank you for being a God that has included us in your family. Thank you that regardless of our rank, race, or reputation, you saved us and loved us. You are a God who is in complete control. Despite our failure, you are faithful. For this, we give you praise. In Jesus' name, amen.

Chapter 7

LESSONS FROM YOUNG LOVERS
(Matthew 1:18-25)

"Now the birth of Jesus Christ was on this wise: When as his mother Mary was espoused to Joseph, before they came together, she was found with child of the Holy Ghost. Then Joseph, her husband, being a just man, and not willing to make her a publick example, was minded to put her away privily. But while he thought on these things, behold, the angel of the Lord appeared unto him in a dream, saying, Joseph, thou son of David, fear not to take unto thee Mary thy wife: for that which is conceived in her is of the Holy Ghost. And she shall bring forth a son, and thou shalt call his name JESUS: for he shall save his people from their sins. Now all this was done, that it might be fulfilled which was spoken of the Lord by the prophet, saying, Behold, a virgin shall be with child, and shall bring forth a son, and they shall call his name Emmanuel, which being interpreted is, God with us. Then Joseph being raised from sleep did as the angel of Lord had bidden him, and took unto him his wife: And knew her not till she had brought forth her firstborn son: and he called his name JESUS."

Eugene Peterson's *The Message* is a paraphrased translation of the Bible, and it reads like this, *"The birth of Jesus took place like this. His mother, Mary, was engaged to be married to Joseph. Before they enjoyed their wedding night, Joseph discovered she was pregnant. (It was by the Holy Spirit, but he didn't know that.) Joseph, chagrined but noble, determined to take care of things quietly so Mary would not be disgraced. While he was trying to figure a way out, he had a dream. God's angel spoke in the dream: "Joseph, son of David, don't hesitate to get married. Mary's pregnancy is Spirit-conceived. God's Holy Spirit has made her pregnant. She will bring a son to birth, and when she does, you, Joseph, will name him Jesus – 'God saves' - because he will save his people from their sins. This would bring the prophet's embryonic sermon to full term: Watch for this - a virgin will get pregnant and bear a son; They will name him Immanuel (Hebrew for 'God is with us'). Then Joseph woke up. He did exactly what God's angel commanded in the dream. He married Mary. But he did not consummate the marriage until she had the baby. He named the baby Jesus. (Matthew 1:18-25)."*

Across the many years and dynasties on the eastern part of the continent of Africa is a village known for producing porcelain and crafting porcelain urns. People come from across the continent of Africa - even the world - to watch these master craftsmen take the porcelain and make urns. The urns are about a table high and a chair wide. One day, in particular, a master craftsman was very meticulously crafting an urn made from porcelain in an East African village. As he was making this beautiful urn, a visitor watched in amazement as the craftsman shaped and molded this material into a great urn. While observing how the craftsman shaped the urn, the craftsman lifted the urn over his head and threw it on the ground, breaking it into many pieces. The visitor who was watching this said, "Oh no! You took that masterpiece, and now it's broken into pieces! What was once beautiful is now broken."

For many, that describes our relationships. They started out beautiful but are now broken. They started out as great masterpieces, but now they are messes. If you would be honest with yourself and roll back the tape of your relationship in your mind, it started out so well. You could not wait to hear his or her voice. Your emotions were heightened, and you were looking forward to seeing him or her. The mention of his or her name and hearing that voice sent a chill up and down your spine. But now, you cannot stand to be in the same room because that is what happens to relationships. Did not the great songstress, the late Minnie Riperton, say, "I stumbled on a photograph; it kinda made me laugh. It took me way back, back down memory lane. I see the happiness. I see the pain. Where am I? Back down memory lane.

I see us standing there, such a happy, happy pair, love beyond compare. Look at there, look at there. The way you held me, no one could tell me that love would die."

That is what happens in relationships. They can start out so good, but they can end up so bad. Life takes your relationships through ups and downs, changes and challenges, and twists and turns. You are now wondering how you can make it through that which was once beautiful - but is now broken; that which was fun - but is now fractured, that which was merry - but is now mess.

If you have ever been there, you can identify with this man in the text by the name of Joseph. Joseph does not say too much, but he has quite a story. He was espoused to the lady of his life, the woman of his dreams, by the name of Mary. She was a young girl. Scholars say she was about 15 or 16 years old. They were in the midst of a beautiful, fairytale relationship until one day, he discovered she was pregnant, and he knew he was not the father. He knew he was not the father because the Bible uses the word "espoused," meaning they were engaged. It was like what we call an engagement, but it was more than an engagement. They had pledged and promised to be together, but they had not consummated the relationship.

This engagement period lasted one year, and Jesus was at the center of it. It started out with Jesus at the center because Mary was pregnant with Jesus. Joseph was a just man, a good man, and a noble man. Mary and Joseph even had some restraint as it related to intimacy. Things appeared to go right. But you can have Jesus in your life, Jesus can be in the center of your relationship, and you can still have some problems. You can be hooked up with someone who has Jesus on the inside. You can even have someone who is noble, righteous, and with great integrity, and problems can still show up in your relationship. That was what was happening with Joseph. He was a good and noble man, hooked up with the woman who had Jesus on the inside, and they still had some problems because she was found to be pregnant, and he knew he was not the father. He figured she had been cheating and unfaithful to him. He was in distress but now look at Joseph's decision. He decided he loved her so much that he would put her away privately.

He said to himself, I don't want to make a public example out of you. I don't want the rumor mill to churn around town or people whispering when you walk down the street. Quietly and privately, we will put an end to this. We will break up. Publicly, we will look like everything is going well, but privately, I'll put you away.

That is where somebody is today. Dr. Jeffrey A. Johnson, says how some relationships can be "publicly united but privately separated." Publicly, it looks like everything is going great, but privately, you have already broken up. You are already divorced. Did you know that it does not start right then when someone gets divorced? Most breakups are not blowouts. They are slow leaks. By the time you find out, you have already been divorced privately. On the outside, you look good. On the outside, you are holding hands. On the outside, you are looking into each other's eyes. On the outside, things are going well. However, there has already been a divorce privately, emotionally, psychologically, and even sexually. And so, that is what Joseph said to himself. He said privately; I just want to put you away.

Then Joseph had a dream, and God began to speak to him because he was getting ready to make a major mistake due to some issues in his relationship. This word is for anyone who has had some problems, some fractures in friendships, some ruptures in relationships, and some mess in your marriage. There is a word for you -- *Before you make a drastic decision, stop and hear what God has to say to you.* This is what God said to Joseph through the angel in a dream: First of all, Joseph, you need to understand Mary has conceived her child of the Holy Ghost. That which is inside Mary was conceived by the Holy Spirit, and she is going to produce it. She is going to bring it to pass.

Now here is what I love about this, sisters. Before Mary connected with Joseph, she already had something in her. Let me help you. *Have something in you before you hook up because you can still produce if it does not work out.* The angel said: Guess what, Joseph, you are getting ready to mess up because the woman you connected to already had something in her before you hooked up with her. If you start tripping and trying to put her down, she will still produce with or without you. Look at what it says in Verse 20, *"for that which is conceived"* (past tense). She had already conceived it in the past. Verse 21 says, *"She shall bring forth"* (future tense). She was hooked up with God, and God had put something in her prior to him. Now you can enjoy each other, and it can be pleasurable, palatable, and productive together, but if you want to trip, she is still going to produce in the future. Please understand this is not to put the brothers down; this is an encouragement for the sisters: No man is looking for a woman who does not have anything, is not doing anything, and is not about anything. Men are looking for women who already have it going on, so when you come together, you bring your tables together. Women, no black knight is riding in on a white horse coming into your neighborhood to save you. We don't roll like that.

Mary had something in her to produce with or without Joseph. There is some stuff you do without a man. Now, this is important for Mary because in Luke 1, when the angel came and told her she would produce something extraordinary that would bless the whole world, she said, how can I do that? How can this be when I don't know a man? The angel told her the Holy Ghost would come upon her and what He would do in her she did not need a man to do. Sisters, you can get saved without a man. You can get filled with the Holy Ghost without a man. You can get that car without a man. You can get that house without a man. You can get that bachelor's degree without a man. You can get that master's degree without a man. You can get that Ph.D. without a man. You can do all that without a man.

Now, let me help the brothers out. Joseph, I know you are hurt and disappointed because you think your girl has been stepping out on you. I get that you are hurt. I get that you are disappointed. But you are getting ready to mess up. You are getting ready to break it off. Wait a minute, Joseph, because this woman has Jesus in her, and if you put her down, who are you picking up? Who are you going to choose when you have someone with Jesus in her?

The angel told Joseph to fear not. Joseph was fearful and afraid. He was afraid to connect and commit. He was afraid to marry her. Wait a minute, Joseph. Do not be fearful of Mary. Mary had Jesus in her. If you are afraid of any woman, Joseph, be afraid of the woman who does not have Jesus on the inside. If she does not have Jesus, there is no telling what she would do. She might be texting you every two minutes. She might be slashing your tires. She might even be outside your job stalking you! There is no telling. The woman who does not have Jesus in her is the one who you need to fear.

I get it, Joseph. You have never met a woman that had Jesus in her. I see why you are afraid. This is the first time you have ever encountered a woman with Jesus on the inside. I see why you are afraid to commit because out of all the marriages you have seen, you are about to have a supernatural marriage. The Holy Ghost is wrapped up in this. Jesus is all a part of this, Joseph. I know you are used to tradition, but this is not going to be natural; it is not going to be ordinary. You know, they say two out of three marriages end in divorce. One out of two marriages in the church end in divorce, so I know you are afraid because you are looking for an ordinary traditional wedding. Well, yours will not be ordinary.

When you get engaged, everything is wonderful. You pick out the wedding colors, you know how many bridesmaids and groomsmen you are going to have, and you spend time gazing into each other's eyes. Everything is wonderful, and the first two or three years of marriage are beautiful. That is traditional; that is normal. Then in about the fourth year of marriage, you cannot stand each other, sleeping in separate rooms and separate beds.

Before you know it, because you will not communicate and work on your issues, you find yourself in divorce court with a lawyer negotiating visitation rights and child support. That is normal and ordinary. But Joseph, there is a difference with your marriage. What is the difference? Jesus is at the center of it. And, when you have Jesus at the center of your marriage, it does not mean you will not have problems. It does not mean you will not get hurt. But Jesus can see you through any issue, any problem, any difficulty, any challenge, any change, any turn. When you have Jesus in your marriage, He makes the difference.

Joseph, are you going to put Mary away? In the second chapter of Matthew, the wise men come, and they bring gold, frankincense, and myrrh. Joseph, you are about to get some gold! You are about to get all these blessings just because you hooked up with the right woman. She is not one you want to put away. This is about your future. Isaiah 7:14 says, *"Behold, a virgin shall be with child, and shall bring forth a son."* This is about their future, and this will fulfill what the prophet had spoken. It is about the plan of God that God prophesied 700 years prior through the Prophet Isaiah. He said a virgin was going to bring forth a son. Joseph, this is about God's plan. I know you are in pain, but you know God can use your intimate pain to weave it into his ultimate plan.

If you are reading this today and in pain, you need to understand that God can weave your intimate pain into fulfilling his ultimate plan for your life. God will take your disappointment and still fulfill His destiny for you. God will take your suffering and your woe and accomplish His sovereign Will for you. That is the kind of God I serve. Even though you go through some pain, it is still to fulfill His perfect will.

So far, I have reviewed *Joseph's decision, Joseph's dream,* and *Joseph's distress.* Finally, let us look at *Joseph's demonstration.* Matthew 1, Verse 24 says, *"Then Joseph being raised from sleep did as the angel of the Lord had bidden him, and took unto him his wife."* He did it, and that is why I like Joseph.

Joseph did not say anything, but he was a man of action. Every time he heard from God, he started moving. He heard from God in Matthew Chapter 1. He got up, married Mary, then in Chapter 2, he got word that Herod was trying to kill all the boys. He heard from God again and took Mary and the boy down to Egypt for safety. He heard from God again and took the boy and Mary back to Jerusalem. Every time he heard from God, he did not say anything. He just moved in the way and the things of God.

God does not just want you to hear what He says; He wants you to do what He says. It is not enough for you to just attend church, sing, shout, hear the word, and then go back the same way, doing the same old thing, with the same attitude you had before. No. God is looking for some change. God does not just want you to be a hearer of the word. He wants you to be a doer of the word. What good is it for you to hear the word and not do it? What good is it do for you to attend Bible study but not follow the word?

Joseph did what God told him to do. He was determined and had already decided that he would put Mary away, but his mind got changed. How do you change the mind of a just man? How do you change the mind of a righteous man? Sisters, let me tell you what not to do. You do not change him by your constant bickering, griping, and complaining. I said a just man. You are engaged or have a boyfriend, and you believe God brought him into your life. You believe you ought to be together, but something has transpired, and it has caused a wedge. You keep trying to change his mind. He is a man of God. He has Jesus in him. He is a just man. How are you going to change him? Or, maybe you are married and have some problems, and you are wondering how you will change it. Notice how Mary did not say anything. The angel spoke. That is what changed Joseph's mind, not Mary. It is not your conversation or your constant nagging that will do it. It was not Mary's conversation that changed Joseph's mind; it was the voice of God.

Now, let me flip it. Dr. John Kenny says this, "Israel continued to cry to God because Israel knew God had what she needed." So, brothers, even though you may not like your woman complaining, as long as she is talking, that means there is hope. You may not like her complaining, but you are in trouble if she ever gets quiet. When a woman stops talking, that means there is no hope and no chance. She is looking for some options.

Joseph woke up, did what God told him to do, and he named the baby Jesus. I like Joseph. The only time he spoke was when he called the name Jesus. He did not say anything else in the whole Christmas story. He only called the child, Jesus. What I also like about Joseph is he was calling Jesus' name after things worked out. Before, things were a little rocky, a little shaky, a little shattering, but then they got married. Things were together, and he still called on the name of Jesus.

Do not just call on Jesus' name while things are in trouble. After things get well, still call on the name of Jesus. Do not wait until trouble comes to call on His name. I need the Lord even when things are going well.

Are you still thinking about that urn in the village of East Africa that the man broke? Are you trying to figure out what happened to that urn when the visitor said, "Oh no!" when he broke it? He broke that urn into all those pieces, and then the master craftsman took all the pieces, took some gold filigree, and began to fill in the broken places of the broken urn. The filigree was not only a design and a decoration, but it became the glue that was able to hold the broken pieces together. He told the visitor that it was fractured but not finished. It was broken, but it was not at its best. He was able to put it together only after it broke, and the filigree was not just a design, but it was the thing holding it together. It was more valuable after it had been broken than it was before.

When life has broken and fractured you, will you let the grace of His filigree fill in your broken pieces? God will fill in that which is broken and take that which is a mess and put it back together again. He can take your broken life, put it back together and make it brand new.

"In case you have fallen by the wayside of life,
dreams and visions shattered, you're all broken inside,
you don't have to stay in the shape that you're in. The Potter
wants to put you back together again.
In case your situation has turned upside down, and all that
you've accomplished is now on the ground, you don't have to
stay in the shape that you're in.
The Potter wants to put you back together again.
You who are broken, stop by the Potter's house.
You who need mending, stop by the Potter's house, give him the
fragments of your broken life."

Do you know the Potter will put you back together again? He will take your brokenness and put you back together. He will take your fracture and finish you with His grace. Just call on the name of Jesus, and He will put you back together again. I know you are broken, but He can put you back. I know you are down, but He can put you back. I know it does not look like you can make it, but He can put you back, and He can do it right now! His grace is filling in the broken places. Do not give up. Do not let the devil have your marriage. Do not let the devil steal your marriage or your family. God will put it back.

Let us pray*:*
Dear Lord, thank you for loving us so much that you sent your son Jesus to save us from our sins. In difficult times and in our phases of disappointment, help us not rush to make drastic decisions and learn to wait quietly for your instructions. Help us to recognize the relationships worth having are the ones already ordained by you in fulfillment of your purpose, plan, and destiny for our lives. I lift up every person whose spirit may be broken and pray that you will put them back together again.

Chapter 8

THAT KIND OF LOVE
(Romans 5:5-11)

"And hope maketh not ashamed; because the love of God is shed abroad in our hearts by the Holy Ghost which is given unto us. For when we were yet without strength, in due time Christ died for the ungodly. For scarcely for a righteous man will one die: yet peradventure for a good man some would even dare to die. But God commendeth his love toward us, in that, while we were yet sinners, Christ died for us. Much more then, being now justified by his blood, we shall be saved from wrath through him. For if, when we were enemies, we were reconciled to God by the death of his Son, much more, being reconciled, we shall be saved by his life. And not only so, but we also joy in God through our Lord Jesus Christ, by whom we have now received the atonement."

Most people have birthmarks specific to them, whether moles or other unique identifying marks. Designers are known by their trademarks. They have logos of various kinds. It is clear who made it even if you don't read the name. God likewise has established a mark, a very clear mark by which his children who have been birthed by the Spirit ought to be known. Love is the birthmark of the believer. Without the birthmark of love, other people really don't know who we are.

Justification is the act of God's impunity, or righteousness charged to our account, which means the wrath that belongs to us went to Jesus, and we attained the grace of God. It is the blessing God gives to the believing sinner declaring us righteous. We are guilty, but God declares us righteous, and because he declares us righteous, He forgives our sin. We are saved from condemnation, and there are five benefits that go along with that.

There was a time when Adam and Eve talked with God. In Genesis Chapter 3, they walked with God face-to-face, but sin turned God's face away from humanity. Through the Savior, Jesus Christ, we have hope. Yes, even though we go through some trials and tribulations, He gives us endurance and strength in the struggle. Endurance gives us approval and character; that character produces hope.

This same principle of virtues is repeated in James 1:2-5, 1 Peter 1:6-7, and by Paul in Romans 5:3-4. Three times James Peter and Paul talk about the link of why we must go through struggle, how struggle makes us strong, and how we are approved after we endure. After we are approved, then we have hope.

That is what the Apostle Paul is lifting up in Verse 5, the love of God. It is immeasurable and immense. Verse 5 says, *"And hope maketh not ashamed."* He was talking about what hope is. What is hope? *H.O.P.E. - Having Only Positive Expectations.* We are not ashamed of it. Why? Because the love of God has been shed abroad in our hearts. The New International Version of the Bible goes on to say in Romans 5:5, *"God's love has been poured out into our hearts through the Holy Spirit"* Because we have the Holy Spirit, it is a testament to the love of God. It is extravagant love. It is abundant love. It is unending love. It is the same word used in Acts 2:17 when Peter was preaching on the day of Pentecost. He quoted the prophet by saying, *"...in the last days, saith God, I will pour out of my Spirit upon all flesh."* That does not mean He is going to leak it out. It is not like an eyedropper. It is like a gush, an overflowing stream. Interestingly, this is the first time the Apostle Paul mentions the Holy Spirit in Romans. In Romans 5:5, he mentions love for the first time also. Of course, he mentions both later in the book. If you ever question the love of God, understand that God's love has not just been dropped on you; it's gushed out. It has been gushed out because God's love is so intense. He has so much love for you; your heart cannot contain it.

I have five empty cups. Imagine they are containers of your heart. I have a pitcher filled with water that represents the love of God. Now, as I pour water from the pitcher into one of the empty cups, this is God's love pouring in. The Apostle Paul explained how you try to contain God's love, but God's love has been poured out. If I keep pouring into the first cup, it is going to overflow. I need another cup. I cannot pour all the water into that cup; I still have some left. That is what happens when God loves you. It just overflows, and you cannot contain it all. After filling up the third, fourth, and fifth cups, I still have water left. Trying to contain the love of God is like trying to hold a gallon of water in an eight-ounce cup.

That is what it is like trying to exhaust the love of God. I do not care what you have done; I do not care what mistakes you have made; I do not care what happened in your life; you cannot exhaust God's love. It has been shed abroad in our hearts. M any non-believers do not know about God's love. God's love has been placed in each one of us. You need to take some of that love and pour it into somebody else. Have you shown love to somebody today? This week, this month? Take that love God has given to you and pour it into somebody else.

That is the love of God, and Paul said one of the benefits we have because we have been justified is we have been indwelled. The Holy Spirit is the spirit of love, and the love of God has been shed abroad in our hearts.

Deaconess Iley Wallace, one of Metropolitan's beloved mothers, used to sing, *"I've Got the Love of Jesus in My Heart."* You have the love. You have it in your heart. It has been shared abroad. You cannot contain it. It is all over us.

2 Corinthians 5:14 says, *"For the love of Christ constraineth us; because we thus judge, that if one died for all, then were all dead."* The love of God constrains us. That means it controls us. When God's love is overflowing in us, it controls our attitude and how we act. You cannot tell me you have the love of God when you are acting hateful toward other people. You cannot tell me you have the love of God, and you treat people nasty. You cannot say you have the love of God when you do not treat your family right, especially people you live with. You are

kind to everyone else outside your home but mean, nasty, evil, and hard to get along with people right there at home. When you have the Holy Spirit, the Holy Spirit will convict your mind and make you apologize when you do someone wrong. The Holy Spirit has been shed abroad in your heart, and that love is demonstrated when you give and when you apologize.

Verse 6 says, *"For when we were yet without strength, in due time Christ died for the ungodly."* What did he do in the past? He died for the ungodly. In the past, Christ died for us. He died for us before we got cleaned up - before we got ourselves together. The Apostle Paul was trying to show us what Christ did for us in the past - not when we got cleaned up, but when we were dirty. He died for us when we were ungodly. Why did He do it? He did it because He loves us.

Verses 7-8 say, *"For scarcely for a righteous man will one die: yet peradventure for a good man some would even dare to die. But God commendeth his love toward us, in that, while we were yet sinners, Christ died for us."* Christ did it while we were still sinners and while we were still enemies of God. That is what He did. See, it is easy to say you will show someone love when they get themselves together. Once they are walking right, then you will show some love. Of course, we can never get right on our own. But God is so gracious, God is so loving, that while we were sinners, Christ died for us. To sin means to aim and miss the mark. We were not even trying to hit the mark. God loved us. God loved you, not when you got cleaned up, but while you were in your sins. Now, who would not serve a God like that? Who would not love a God like that?

That was the past. Now, look at God's present work. Verse 9 says, *"Much more then, being now justified by his blood."* Justified - *just as if I'd never sinned*. You are justified just as if you never sinned, by Christ's blood, and because of that, we shall be saved from the wrath through Him. That means you are safe from hell. Hell is real, and we are saved from hell, from the wrath. Why is that? Because the wrath of God that was coming toward us went to Jesus. He poured his wrath on Jesus and shed His blood because of His love for us. That is the act of justification. That is the result of justification.

Verse 10 says, *"For if, when we were enemies, we were reconciled to God by the death of his Son, much more, being reconciled, we shall be saved by his life."* It is as if Jesus was on the cross, and one hand was holding the hand of God while the other hand was holding the hand of humanity. He was putting us back together. Sin pulled us apart, but with His stretched hands on the cross, He took the hand of God with one hand and the hand of humanity, and He put us back together. I know it was an awful strain because He did it with nails in His hands. But He reconciled us back to God. Much more, being reconciled, we shall be saved by His life. Presently, He preserves you; He is keeping you. In other words, the same God that saved you can keep you. Do not think that you serve a God that will leave you.

Someone who is reading this today is in a difficult dilemma right now. But understand that the same God that saved you is able to keep you in every circumstance, in every issue, and every problem. He is able to keep you. Paul said, *"I know in whom I have believed, and am persuaded that he is able to keep that which I have committed unto him (2 Timothy 1:12)."* Not only is He able to keep you from falling and to present you faultless before his presence with exceeding joy, but He is also able to keep you even when you do not want to be kept. You wanted to go somewhere and do the wrong thing. He said - no, no, no. He kept you. Right now, you can thank God for His keeping power, that He keeps you, and He does it whether you want to be kept or not. You wanted to stray to the left or stray to the right, and He said - No. I'm going to keep you.

The Psalmist picked it up in Psalm 121, *"He that keepeth Israel shall neither slumber nor sleep."* Why are you worrying? Go to sleep! I decided that since God is going to be up anyway, there is no sense in the both of us being up all night. Since He will be up anyway, I will just fluff my pillow, and I will just go to sleep. He's keeping Israel; He does not sleep nor slumber. If He can keep Israel - He can keep you. If He keeps Israel - He will keep your job. If He keeps Israel - He will keep your family. If He keeps Israel - He can keep your son, daughter, and grandchildren. He is able to keep you!

God's eyes are on you, and He declares us righteous. Verse 11 says, *"And not only so, but we also joy in God through our Lord Jesus Christ, by whom we have now received the atonement."* We are as one now through Jesus Christ. That is the love of God. God's love is endless; it does not change. Nothing you can do will exhaust the love of God.

What are the five benefits that we have from being justified according to Romans 5:1-11?

1) We have peace with God. We have been justified, so now we are at peace with him. Peace with God means we are able to have the peace of God.

2) We have access to God. We can go boldly to the throne in the presence of God.

3) We even have the assurance of God. Even though we go through some tough times, it does not mean we are not going to have to suffer because we have the *peace of God,* the *pardon of God* in the *presence of God.* We are still going to go through some issues and problems. But if we have the peace of God on the inside, we can handle the pressures of life on the outside.

4) We are indwelled by God through His Holy Spirit, and it is shed abroad. I cannot even contain it any more than the little cup in my demonstration can contain it. You cannot contain the love of God because it is in you. It ought to flow out of you.

5) And finally, we are preserved by God. The same God that saved us through the precious love of Jesus is able to keep us.

Let us pray:

Thank you, LORD, for the kind of love that is shed abroad in our hearts. Your loving kindness and tender mercies are beyond our comprehension. We are so thankful that nothing can remove us from the divine love you have for us through Christ Jesus. In Jesus' name. Amen.

Chapter 9

ENDLESS LOVE
(Romans 8:38)

"For I am persuaded that neither death, nor life, nor angels, nor principalities, nor powers, nor things present, nor things to come, nor height, nor depth, nor any other creature, shall be able to separate us from the love of God, which is in Christ Jesus our Lord."

The movie from 1981, "Endless Love," starring Brooke Shields, was not received well by critics; and was not publicly received. It was actor Tom Cruise's first time in a film. He had a minor part but what was popular was the song "Endless Love" written by Lionel Richie, which he performed with Diana Ross. It spent nine weeks at number one on the charts. It received five Grammy nominations, Golden Globe, and Academy Award nominations. But the real endless love is not on the screen, and it is not in a song. The actual description of endless love is found in the Scriptures.

The Apostle Paul shares with us that there is nothing that will separate us from the love of God. The real endless love is the love that God has for you. God has an endless, undying love for you. What is awesome about God's love is that He cannot love you any more than He loves you right now. It is an endless love; it is a love that nothing can separate, nothing can stop, and nothing can sway.

At the end of Chapter 7 in the Book of Romans, Paul talks about his struggle between doing what he ought to do and doing what he did not want to do. He said in verse 19, *"For the good that I would I do not: but the evil which I would not, that I do."* He goes on to say in Verse 21, *"...when I would do good, evil is present."* He was struggling. He was wrestling with his desire to please God and the struggle of his flesh that displeases God. In Verse 24, he said, *"Oh wretched man that I am! who will deliver me from the body of this death."* He talked about his struggle, but we all have that struggle. There are days when we are walking and living for God, and then there are other days when we are wrestling and struggling. We all struggle like the apostle Paul, but the good news is that the struggle will not separate us. Even though we go through some struggles internally, there is no separation.

Notice the vision of crisis that the Apostle Paul describes to us in Romans 8:35. He raised the query, *"Who shall separate us from the love of Christ?"* Then he nominated some things: *"Shall tribulation, or distress, persecution, famine, nakedness, and his peril, or sword?"* He said in Verse 36, *"As it is written, for thy sake we are killed all the day long; we are accounted as sheep for the slaughter."* The metaphor he used to describe followers of Christ is "sheep ready for the slaughter." When you make a decision to stand for God, when you make a decision to stand for Christ, you are saying, Lord, I'll do what you want me to do; I'll say what you want me to say; I'll go where you tell me to go. Whenever you do that, you are a target. If you are not trying to do something and have something and be something for God, nobody is against you. As soon as you raise up your head and start walking through the door that God gives you, adversaries and enemies will be there to pull you down. The description is that you are sheep prepared for the slaughterhouse.

Do not be alarmed when people start talking about you or things start to go haywire when you *up* your commitment with Christ. Do not be surprised when you start to go through some things once you become diligent about praying, fasting, and reading God's word. When you become serious about doing the will of God and following His plan and purpose for your life, you are recognized as sheep for the slaughterhouse. But the good news is the slaughter will not separate us! Paul started naming some things, "Who shall separate us from the love of Christ?" Shall persecution, or distress, or tribulation or nakedness? Each one of these things he names intensifies in degree. It starts with persecution, but then it ends with the sword, which is to kill. It begins with just wanting to hurt you, but it ends with wanting to destroy you. Satan is not out to hurt your feelings. Satan is not out just to make you feel bad. Satan wants to destroy you, but in Romans 8:39, Paul said, *"nothing shall be able separate us from the love of God, which is in Christ Jesus our Lord."*

The Book of Romans comes before 1 and 2 Corinthians in the Bible. But, chronologically, 1 and 2 Corinthians were written before Romans. They were written in A.D. 55 and Romans in A.D. 56. For you great mathematicians, you know that 55 comes before 56. Paul said nothing would be able to separate us from the love of Christ, not even these things: persecution, distress, tribulation, famine, nakedness, peril, or sword. That was what was about to happen. But 1 and 2 Corinthians were written before Romans. Why is that important? In 2 Corinthians Chapter 11, Paul outlined some things he had already gone through. He said he had already been beaten three times. He had been beaten five times by the Jews. He had been persecuted. He had been abandoned. He had nakedness in his life, and he had peril and sword. He had been through shipwrecks and problems in the wilderness. He said it got so bad that the governor of Damascus shut down the city so that he could arrest Paul and persecute him. But by God's providence, some people had mercy on Paul and let him out of a window in a basket. He was a basket case because of all the stress he was going through.

In Romans 8, Paul talked about things that could separate him, but he knew nothing like that would separate him because he had already been through it. In other words, he looked back on his life and said, I've already been through persecution. That didn't separate me. I've already been through tribulation. That didn't separate me. I've already been through peril and sword and nakedness and famine. It didn't separate me back then, so I don't have to worry about what is coming in my future because all of that stuff had a chance to separate me. I have been through it, and now I can rejoice because nothing will separate me from the love of Christ Jesus.

Every now and then, you need to look back on what you have already been through, and when you look back, you can say, like Paul, it will never separate you. Why? Because it has already had a chance.

The divorce did not separate you.
Unemployment did not separate you.
Issues with your finances did not separate you.
Problems with your children did not separate you.

If that didn't separate you, you do not have to worry about what will happen in your future because it already had a chance, and you are still here. Think about what you have already been through that would have separated you; it could have separated you, and maybe it should have separated you, but because of the goodness of God, it could not separate you from the love of Jesus!!!

That is the vision of crisis but watch the victory of the conqueror. It says right there in Romans 8:37, *"Nay, in all these things we are more than conquerors through him that loved us."* He gives us, first of all, the circumference of our confidence. He says, *"in all these things,"* not from all, but in all. Your victory is not from all; it is in all. You think your victory is the things you avoided, the problems you escaped, or the trouble that didn't happen to you, but Paul is here to let you know your conquering is in all.

We look at Noah because he sailed through the flood and not around the flood. The children of Israel were delivered, not from the wilderness, but in the wilderness. The three Hebrew boys were not delivered from the fire; they were delivered right in the midst of the fire. Daniel was delivered not from the lions' den but in the lions' den. I am just here to let you know that your trouble, your pain, your victory is not *from all* these things, but *in all* these things. In the midst of what you are going through, you can still have the victory. I always say, "what God doesn't deliver you from, he'll deliver you in, and he'll deliver you through." You've been in the midst of it, but in it, you are a conqueror.

Paul said in all these things; we are currently conquering. We are more than conquerors - not want to be, not trying to be, not hoping to be, but we are. You ought to just say, "I am a conqueror right now."

Even in the midst of your sickness, you are a conqueror.

Right in the middle of your financial problems, you are a conqueror.

Right in the midst of your heartache, you are a conqueror.

Right in the midst of that enemy trying to slow you down, trying to stop you, trying to hurt you, you are more than a conqueror.

You are more than a conqueror through Jesus Christ who loves you. But you are not just a conqueror; you are more than a conqueror! The Greek word *Nikeo* is where we get the word, "Nike." Nike is an athletic company known for its clothing, athletic shoes, and sporting goods. Nike is an athletic term because conquerors are those who compete and win, but those who are more than conquerors are those who dominate their particular sport. There are conquerors, and then there are more than conquerors.

That happened in sports such as basketball in the 1960s. The Boston Celtics won the championship 10 out of 12 years. They dominated the 60s. In the 80s, it was the Lakers. Out of 10 years, they had five championship titles. In the 90s, the Chicago Bulls won six out of 10 championships series. The Celtics, the

Lakers, and the Bulls were not just conquerors; they were more than conquerors. That is what God is trying to say about you. You are not just a conqueror; you are more than a conqueror. Do you know why? Because just when it seems like you have given all you have, you get some more strength. Just when it seems like you have given all you can, you got some more power. Just when it seems like you prayed all you can pray, you can pray some more. You are more than a conqueror. Can you rejoice because you are more than a conqueror? Can you give God praise because you are more than a conqueror?

That is the *vision of crisis* and the *victory of the conqueror*. Finally, there is the *voice of confidence*. In Romans 8:38, Paul said, *"Now I am persuaded."* See, once you have been through something, once God has delivered you, once God has made a way for you, you can speak with some confidence. Once you have been through some persecution, some trouble, some peril, and some sword, you can say I am persuaded; I am confident about this and about that.

I am thoroughly convinced that nothing can separate you, not death nor life, nor angels, nor principalities, nor powers, nor things present, nor things to come; nor height, nor depth, nor any other creature will be able to separate you from the love of God that is in Christ Jesus.

Let me tell you something about His love:

> His love is so awesome!
> His love is so amazing!
> His love is so phenomenal!
> No rules can restrict it!
> No words can explain it!
> No theory can contain it!
> No tyrant can prevent it!
> No adversary can allude to it!
> No sickness will overwhelm it!

No death can overcome it!
No enemy can overthrow it!
No weapon can overtake it!
No pressure can delete it!
No problem can depress it!
No power can defeat it!
No fire can burn it!
No water can drown it!
No dirt can cover it!
No trouble can topple it!
No time can erase it!

Nothing will be able to separate you from the love of God that is in Christ Jesus. I don't know about you, but I thank God for his love. Aren't you glad that God loves you!

Let us pray:

Dear Lord, thank you for loving us with an endless love. Thank you for the assurance that nothing will be able to separate us from your love and the love that is in Christ Jesus. Help us to remember that we are not just conquerors but are more than conquerors.

Chapter 10

LOVE'S POWER OVER ALL THINGS
I Corinthians 13:1-7

"Though I speak with the tongues of men and of angels and have not charity, I am become as sounding brass or a tinkling cymbal. And though I have the gift of prophecy, and understand all mysteries and all knowledge, and though I have all faith, so that I could remove mountains, and have not charity, I am nothing. And though I bestow all my goods to feed the poor, and though I give my body to be burned, and have not charity. It profiteth me nothing. Charity suffereth long and is kind, charity envieth not; charity vaunteth not itself, is not puffed up, Doth not behave itself unseemly, seeketh not her own, is not easily provoked, thinketh no evil; Rejoiceth not in iniquity, but rejoices in the truth; Beareth all things, believeth all things, hopeth all things, endureth all things."

Dr. Tony Evans tells the story of a woman who had a husband who kept a list. This list contained 25 things he wanted her to do to be a good wife for him. Every day, he took out the list and checked off the things she completed. Cooking - check, cleaning – check, care of the kids – check. At the end of the day, he would let her know how she scored. She had 23 out of 25, 21 out of 25, etc. This woman was miserable. She was miserable because she didn't marry to be tied to a checklist. Not that the things she did as a wife weren't important. They were important and necessary, but she had higher hopes for her marriage relationship.

After several years the husband died. The woman felt a weight lifted from her shoulders because she had been performing for years. She had been doing her duty and hating every minute even though the duties themselves weren't innately bad. Two years later, the same woman fell in love with a new guy, a guy who had no list. He told this woman that all he wanted to do was to love her. He wanted her to wake up in the morning knowing that he loved her. In the middle of the day, he wanted to be able to call and remind her that he loved her. At night before they retired, he wanted to reassure her that he loved her. He wanted his love for her to be her every waking thought of her day. He wanted her to know his love, not his list. One day she was cleaning the house; she opened up her drawer and saw a piece of paper. It was the list from the first husband. She giggled when she realized that everything written down, all 25 duties, were happening effortlessly in her new marriage. Everything her husband graded her on in her first marriage, she was doing for her second husband and loving it. All the second husband had was love. It brought joy to this woman, her home, and all she did for it. She was overpowered by love.

When the Apostle Paul begins to talk about love (charity) in 1 Corinthians 13, he starts with some negative things to describe what love is not. He says love is not envious; it is not angry, it is not prideful, it is not rude, and it is not bitter. But then Paul shifts in Verse 7 to some very positive things about love and how it is demonstrated and practiced. He says love bears all things, believes all things, hopes all things, and endures all things. What is intriguing is not these verbs, as strong as they are - bear, believe, hope, and endure - but it is the reoccurring theme of all things. In other words, no matter the situation or circumstance, whatever things you may be dealing with, love can be applied because it bears all things, believes all things, hopes all things, and endures all things. It does not matter what you are facing; it does not matter what condition you may find yourself in; love can be appropriated. It is universal. I know it is universal because when God had a universal problem of sin, He commended His love toward us, and while we were yet sinners, Christ died for us. So, no matter what it is, you can face all things with the power of love.

Scripture says love bears all things. That word *bear* is like the picture of a roof that does not leak, so solid that it holds things up and keeps them up, so there is not a leak. It means it is able to shelter us through storms. It is able to keep us covered and not exposed to bad things, which is important because we live in a society that enjoys a scandal. You cannot get past the checkout line in the grocery store without seeing tabloids with stories of this person breaking up that person. That person is going out with this person and so on. Society gravitates to that stuff. But love bears all things - BEARS all things, not BARES as in, exposes all things. That is what the world does. But love bears it, covers it, seals it up, and it does not let it leak out.

Not only does love bear all things, it believes all things. It does not mean love is gullible. It means love always seeks to find the best in the person or the predicament. I am glad about that because that is what God does for us. He looks for the best in us. God seeks to find the best and the most positive qualities in us. God sees more in us than we can even see. And even though you have messed up, even though you have some issues, God still wants to use you!

Abraham and Sarah were too old.
Jeremiah was too young.
Paul had a thorn in his flesh.
Peter denied Jesus.
James and John had anger issues.
Jonah was a prophet on the run.
Isaiah said he was unclean and undone.

And yet, God used all of them because He sees the best in us. He believes all things, and that is what love does; it believes all things. Love hopes all things. Dr. Kevin Cosby, the Senior Pastor of Saint Stephen Baptist Church in Louisville, Kentucky, said, "Hope is a positive expectation from the God that makes us wait." That is what hope is. It means even though the circumstances around me may seem contradictory, I have a hope of a positive expectation. Sometimes you have to hope against hope. Sometimes, when situations look so bad, you have to hope against them, but you have to have hope because love hopes all things.

Love bears all things, it believes all things, it hopes all things, and then it endures all things. In other words, it keeps going. The word *endure* is a military term that speaks of an army that has come to a territory, staked its claim, and will not move. It means endure until the end, which is important because the race is not given to the swift, nor the battle to the strong, but to the one who endures until the end. It is the power to be able to stick to it. It is to be able to have the strength to keep going. Is that not what Jesus did? He endured the cross, and He despised the shame. That is how I know I can make it because if I ever feel like I am about to give up, I can just look at my Savior, who endured the cross and despised the shame. I know I can make it because weeping may endure for a night, but joy comes in the morning, and the Lord is good despite what I am going through. His mercy is everlasting, and His truth - there it is again - *endures* to *all* generations. That is what love does.

Love bears when it is unbearable. Love believes the unbelievable, and love hopes when things look hopeless. And, if all that does not work, I just endure. If I cannot bear and it seems like I am about to break under the load; if I cannot believe because the situation looks unbelievable, and if I cannot even hope because it looks like everything is hopeless, I just stand there and endure. I cannot hope anymore. I cannot bear anymore. I cannot even believe anymore. So what am I going to do? I am going to just stick it out. I am going to endure. I am just going to stand right here until He comes through. It is the all-encompassing phrase of *all things* that really pulls this love theme together.

Paul wants us to understand that no matter what it is, it is *all things*. Whether it is bearing, whether it is believing, whether it is hoping, whether it is enduring, it is all things. Paul initially said this to the church in Corinth in 1 Corinthians Chapter 3, when they were fighting about which preacher was the best. Some said Apollos was better, some said Cephas was better, and some said

Paul was better. Paul said, why limit yourself? All things are yours. He said Cephas is yours, Paul is yours, Apollos is yours, and Christ is yours because Christ is God's. He told them not to get caught up in limiting themselves and pigeonhole themselves because all things were theirs. Then, in 1 Corinthians 13, Paul said love bears all things, love believes all things, love hopes all things, and love endures all things.

There are times when I try to believe, but even in believing, it appears that my belief is fading away. There are times when I try to hope, but I still have some hopeless situations. And yes, I am trying to endure, but sometimes I feel like giving up. How can I have this love that will keep me going through all things?

Paul picks up this theme again with the church of Rome. Romans 8:28 - my life verse - summarizes and capitalizes my testimony. *Romans 8:28-29 says, "And we know that all things work together for good to them that love God, to them who are the called according to his purpose. For whom he did foreknow, he also did predestinate to be conformed to the image of his Son, that he might be the firstborn among many brethren."*

Paul is saying the reason why love can be applied to all things is because you know all things work together for good to them who love God and to them who are the called according to his purpose. Notice the positive influence of this promise. He said, *and we know.* That is important because what often stresses us out is not what we know but what we do not know. It is what I do not know that stresses me. I do not know if my job will be downsized and if I will get a pink slip. I do not know what the report from the doctor actually means. I do not know if I have enough tuition to finish the semester in school. And in Verse 26, it says sometimes we do not even know what to pray for. You may be a great prayer warrior, but life will throw you some curves and some twists and turns, and you do not even know what to pray for! I do not know whether to ask God to save them or take them. I do not know whether I should ask God to take me to this city or that city. I do not even know what to pray for. There are so many things that we do not know; this is an unknown factor.

However, we do know all things work together for good to them who love God and to them who are the called according to his purpose. The word *know* is interesting because, in the Greek language, you have the word *oida*. So he is saying, I know, I *oida*. This *know* is different from the *know* Paul writes about in Philippians 3:10, which is the word *ginosko* (which means intimately), and *oida* is an ongoing continuous type of knowledge. Paul says in *Philippians 3:10, "That I may know him, and the power of his resurrection, and the fellowship of his sufferings, being made conformable unto his death."* That *know* is an ongoing, continuous, progressive experience, and based on that progressive continuous experience. But this *know* (oida) in Romans 8 is different from that *know (ginosko.)* This *know* is not based on some future experience by which I'll gain future knowledge. This *know*, this *oida* means that I have this knowledge based on past reflection and past experience with God. Paul is saying the reason why I have this confidence is because I can look back over my life, and, based on past experiences, reflect on what God has brought me through. He says l *oida; I* know that all things will work out for my good.

Paul could understand this because he had been shipwrecked, beaten five times, had 39 lashes each time with a whip, stoned, and even stabbed in the back by other ministers. But he said through all of that, I *oida*. I know, based on past experience that all things are working together for my good.

That is what happened with David. He is another witness. There was this nine-foot-six-inch giant named Goliath, and Goliath was going to fight against the Nation of Israel, but nobody would fight him. Then David came along, a little 17-year-old boy, and said, I'll fight him. The people said, You're going to fight him? He said, yes, I will fight him. They said, we have to go tell the King. So they went and got King Saul and said, Saul, we have somebody who will fight the champion Goliath. King Saul looked at him and said, son, this is a champion; this is a giant. This is a nine-foot-six-inch giant. He will stomp you! You can't beat him! David said, I *oida*. I *know* I can beat him. And Saul said, well how do you *oida* that you can? How do you know that? He said, I *oida* because I was in the field with my father's sheep one day, and a lion and a bear tried to kill my father's sheep. And, the spirit of God came all over me and gave me the power to defeat that lion and that bear. I *oida* that God is able to deliver me from this uncircumcised Philistine!

You can look over your life and see some valleys that God brought you through. You can look in your past and see some battles you have fought and some victories God has allowed you to win. And, when you look at your circumstances right now, you can look back and say I *oida*, I know that all things work together for good!

Let me give you another witness. There was a blind man in John Chapter 9. Jesus took some mud and put it on his eyes. I know that would have messed the optometrist up right then. Jesus told the man to go and wash in the Pool of Siloam. He was blind and had mud on his eyes, and Jesus told him to go and wash in a pool? So, the blind man did what Jesus told him to do, and all of a sudden, he was able to see. The Pharisees were mad, and they wanted to get something on Jesus. Because Jesus healed the blind man on the Sabbath day, they said to the man; we know this man is a sinner. The man said, I don't *oida*. I don't know. Whether He be a sinner or not, I don't *oida*. All I *oida* is that I was blind, but now I can see.

You ought to be able to look over your life and see some things God has brought you through. You ought to be able to see the miracles and the ways He has made. I am talking about that time you did not know how you were going to make it, and all of a sudden God came through for you. When you look back at that, you can say to yourself, I know that all things work together for good for those that love God and are called according to His purpose. All things do not look good, and all things do not feel good, and all things do not seem good, but God gets in everything, and He starts working it out for my good!

Has God ever worked anything out for your good? Has God ever come through for you? Has God ever done anything for you and worked it out for your purpose? If yes, then you ought to give Him praise! You can look at your problem and say, I can make it. I can take it because of what I've been through.

I do not know about you, but I have a God-confidence because I have been through the storm and the rain. I thank God for my mountains. I thank God for the storms He brought me through. If I had never had a problem, I would not know that God could solve it. I would not know what faith in God could do. But through it all, I have learned to trust in Jesus. I have learned to trust in God. I have been through trouble, but I thank God He has been with me. I thank God that in the storms, He has been with me. Through the rain, He has been with me. I never would have made it, I never could have made it, and I never should have made it without the Lord. As I look back over my life, I realize I am stronger, wiser, and better because of what I have been through in my life. If it had not been for the Lord on my side, I would not be here today.

Right now, I can say thank you, Lord because you worked it out. When I could not figure it out, the Lord kept working it out. I did not know how I was going to make it, but through it all, I can trust in the Lord.

So, I am just going to trust in the Lord and be of good courage. I am just going to wait on the Lord and watch Him renew my strength. I am just going to wait on the Lord until I mount up on wings like eagles until I run and not get weary until I walk and I do not even faint. I am going to trust in the Lord, who is my light and my salvation. The Lord is the strength of my life; of whom shall I be afraid? When my enemies, even my foes, came to eat up my flesh, they stumbled and fell. The host encamps against them. In this will I be comforted. *One thing have I desired of the Lord and that will I seek after, that I may dwell in the house of the*

Lord forever. For in the time of trouble, He shall hide me in the secret of His tabernacle, in the secret of His pavilion (Psalm 27). Won't He do it?

Let us pray:

Father, right now, in the name of Jesus, thank you for the battles you fought, the victories you won. Thank you for the ways you made. God, we don't approach any situation brand new, but we face it with God-confidence, knowing that if you've blessed us in the past, you can do it now. We approach it knowing that you are able to fix every situation, so God, we just place it in your hands. God, there's so much that we don't know. Sometimes we don't even know what to pray for. We don't know how certain circumstances will work out. But, based on what we do know, we walk, and we bear all things, we believe all things, we hope all things, and we will endure. We will stick with it, Lord. And we thank you for it. We thank you for victory. We thank you that you worked it out, and Lord, we thank you for your purpose. Your divine purpose is being manifested in our lives. Even now, you're shaping us, and you're molding us to fit your divine purpose, and we thank you for it. You are the Potter, we are the clay, so mold us and make us after your will. In Jesus, name, we say hallelujah and amen.

Chapter 11

LOVE'S POWER OVER TIME
I Corinthians 13, 14:1

1 Corinthians: 13:1-13 (NJKV) - Though I speak with the tongues of men and of angels, but have not love, I have become sounding brass or a clanging cymbal. And though I have the gift of prophecy, and understand all mysteries and all knowledge, and though I have all faith, so that I could remove mountains, but have not love, I am nothing. And though I bestow all my goods to feed the poor, and though I give my body to be burned, but have not love, it profits me nothing. Love suffers long and is kind; love does not envy; love does not parade itself, is not puffed up; does not behave rudely, does not seek its own, is not provoked, thinks no evil; does not rejoice in iniquity, but rejoices in the truth; bears all things, believes all things, hopes all things, endures all things. Love never fails. But whether there are prophecies, they will fail, whether there are tongues, they will cease; whether there is knowledge, it will vanish away. For we know in part and we prophesy in part. But when that which is perfect has come, then that which is in part will be done away. When I was a child, I spoke as a child, I understood as a child, I thought as a child; but when I became a man, I put away childish things. For now we see in a mirror, dimly, but then face to face. Now I know in part, but then I shall know just as I also am known. And now abide faith, hope, love, these three; the greatest of these is love.

Chapter 14:1 (NKJV) - Pursue love, and desire spiritual gifts, but especially that you may prophesy. Chapter 13:8 says love never fails. I want to talk about *love's power over time.*

When I was a senior in high school, I had the privilege of going to Madrid, Spain, for the World Expo. One of the first things they told us when we got off the plane was to immediately find a currency exchange center to exchange American money for Spanish money. They said the American dollar was a different type of currency and had a different value in Spain. Because I was in a different location, the value of my money was not the same in this new location as it was when I was here in the states. The value had gone down because I shifted and went to a different place.

The phrase *"Love never fails"* in 1 Corinthians 13:8 literally means love does not lose its value. It means that it does not lose its value regardless of the situation or our location. The value never goes down; the value is never depleted or decreased.

The Apostle Paul was trying to get the truth across to the Church of Corinth. The Church of Corinth was a church that triumphed. They had triumphed in this church because they were saints. Paul called them saints. That was their position. They were saints because they were sanctified. They were set apart for the purposes and plans of God, so they were a triumphant church. This church had tremendous potential. They were gifted, having spiritual gifts and operating in them. They had Speaking gifts, service gifts, and all types of spiritual gifts. They were a very gifted church. Paul tells them in 1 Corinthians 3:21, "a*ll things are yours."* They could possess all things because they were such a wonderful church, a gifted church that triumphed.

The Church of Corinth also had trouble in the church. Even though they had gifts, they did not have any gains. They had potential but not the peace of God. There was fracture in the fellowship. There was a rupture in their relationships. They were caught up in sordid sexual sins and brought lawsuits against the saints.

It was a problematic church that had issues, and that is why Paul says *love bears all things*. The word bear is like a roof that will not leak. Certain things had leaked out in this church. The problem with a leak is even if you fix it, the damage is already done. Things had leaked out to Paul of certain activities that were going on in this church. To combat the trouble in the church, Paul brought some truth to this church because whenever a church has some trouble in it, it must face the truth.

Paul started writing some truth to the church, and the truth he wanted to get across to them was love is the paramount priority. In this overarching discussion on gifts in Chapters 12 and 14, right in between is Chapter 13, and the lessons about love, which says that at the center of everything we do for God, love ought to be there. Whatever we do for the church or someone else, if love is not the motivating factor, its value is nothing, and it profits us nothing.

Watch how Paul did that. He was so clear and precise. In verses 1-3, he talks about the *priority of love*. He wants to convey that regardless of what we do - our activity - love should be our attitude. So many of us are caught up in what we do, but what we are is just as important as what we do. That is why he says though I speak with the tongues of men and of angels but have not love, it profits me nothing. Though I give my body to be burned; though I give everything to the poor; though I have faith that I can move mountains, If I don't have love, it profits me nothing.

He moves from the *priority of love* to the *practice of love*. In Verses 4-7, he explains how we are to live love out in our daily lives. He talks about how love is patient, love is kind, love rejoices in the truth, love bears all things, believes all things, and hopes all things. He talks about how love is always looking with expectation. Love always believes, always bears; it always has a heart of expectation. Paul then tells us what love is not. He says love is not envious. Love is not jealous. Love is not rude; it's not selfish. Love does not get on the phone and gossip. Love is not caught up in itself; it is not puffed up. Love is practiced by patience, by kindness, and by rejoicing in the truth.

In Verse 8, Paul shifts again and moves from the *practice of love*. Having already established the *priority of love*, he talks about the *permanence of love*. Paul expounds on how this love, which is such a priority and is to be practiced in our lives, can withstand the test of time. The value of this love, he says will never fail. In other words, it will always keep its value. The Amplified Bible says *"love never fails (it never fades or ends)."* The Moffat Translation says *"love never disappears."* The Phillips translation says *"love knows no limit to its endurance."* The Message Bible says *love never dies*. In other words, love never goes out of style.

We may fail, but God's love will never fail. That is a reason to rejoice! The love of God is so powerful; it is so poignant, it is so far-reaching that it cannot fail. Paul says in Verse 13 that *"And now abideth faith, hope, love, these three; but the greatest of these three is love"* because sometimes attributes may fall short, but love will keep on going. It is awesome to know the divine love of God will never fail us. This is good because sometimes, human relationships do not always last. Some people can like you today and love you today, but if you do something they do not like, they will not love you next week. Thank God His love is not like human love! It is not inconsistent. It does not go all over the scale. He has a consistent type of love, and His love will not fail. Regardless of what situation you are in, irrespective of your condition, no matter where you are in life, because of the character of God, His love will not fail.

Now abide faith, hope, and love. The attributes of faith are my response to what God has done. Now abide hope. But the greatest of these is love because sometimes my faith will run out. Jesus said to Simon, Satan desires to have you, that he may sift you like wheat. Satan has asked permission to come after you, and he has asked permission to get you and sift you like wheat. But do not worry about it because I prayed for you, and I prayed that your faith fail not. I did not pray that you would not fail because I know you will deny me three times, but I prayed that your *faith* fail not. If Jesus prayed that his faith would not fail, that means there is the potential for faith to fail. So, the attribute of faith can fail us.

Now abideth faith, hope, and love. Every now and then, if you are expecting something and it takes too long to get here, your hope, and your expectation may run out. But when faith runs out of gas and when hope gives out, love is just getting started. For the greatest of these is love. You may run out of faith, and hope may stop expecting, but love says I will always be here. I do not care how bad it gets. I do not care how difficult it seems. I do not care how bad the storm is; love will remain. It will not fail, and it will not fall. Is that not why Paul prayed that the church, the Christians of Ephesus, would be rooted and grounded in love, that they may be able to comprehend the width, length, depth, and height of God's love?

God's love has no boundaries. It has no parameters. It matters not where you go. You can change cities, you can change places, and all you are going to do is run smack dab into the love of God. God loves us so much that even if we try to get away from Him, all we will do is run into His love. God's love is always around you.

The psalmist said it like this in Psalm *139 (NIV) – Where can I go from your Spirit? Where can I flee from your presence? If I go up to the heavens, you are there; If I make my bed in the depths, you are there. If I rise on the wings of the dawn, if I settle on the far side of the sea, even there your hand will guide me, your right hand will hold me fast.*-I cannot get away from God's love. He is everywhere, everywhere I turn, everywhere I go, I am facing the love of God. And the thing about this love is it will not run out. Love is a Fruit of the Spirit, and it is self-regenerating. That is why Paul says gifts will fade. Knowledge is going to fade. The gift of prophecy is going to fade. The gift of tongues is going to fade. Love will always be here because it regenerates itself. When you think you have run out of it, there is something about love that gives you the energy to keep on loving even when you have to love folks that are not always lovely. Something about love prompts you to keep on loving even when it seems like you have expended all of your love.

There have been times when I have gone to the hospital or the nursing home to visit church members or family. I have gone out of love for them. But the more I stayed with them and talked with them; they ended up cheering me up, encouraging me, and helping me out. That is what love does; it regenerates itself. It gives you energy. You cannot use up all of God's love.

You cannot go so low that his love cannot reach down and lift you up. You cannot stray so far that his love cannot find you and pull you back. You cannot escape the love of God.

The late R&B singer Rick James was born, lived, and is buried in Buffalo, New York. He recorded such hits as "Mary Jane," "Superfreak," and "Ebony Eyes." He had an extensive music catalog reportedly worth millions of dollars. While he was a Grammy winner, talented singer, songwriter, and producer, Rick James struggled with drug addiction. It is reported that he would party and overspend money to the point where he would go broke and have no money. Royalties from his music earned him thousands and hundreds of thousands of dollars that he would obtain in checks from his mailbox. He would then use the money to buy drugs and party. This cycle left him broke and unable to pay his bills. When MC Hammer used his song "Super Freak" as a baseline in "U Can't Touch This," he received even more money in royalties because the song was so popular. We can even hear it today in the background of many commercials.

If Rick James could never run out of royalties from "Super Freak," how much will God's love never fail. His love is never finished. The love of God has no expiration date on it. It can never run out. It is always going to be here. John 13:1 says that Jesus, knowing His hour was at hand, called his disciples, for He loved them until the end. He loved them until the end, but one would deny him, another one would betray him, and the rest of them would forsake him. But the Scripture said he loved them until the end, no matter what they did to Him.

A few years ago, Lady Angela and I were back home in Indianapolis, and we took our niece, Breanna, out. Lady Angela wanted to go shopping, so I dropped her off at the store, and she told me just to take Breanna around. Breanna and I drove around, and then she said, "Where's Auntie Angie?" I said, "Auntie Angie went shopping." "I want to see Auntie Angie," Breanna said. I said, "She's shopping, and we're driving around. The purpose for her leaving you is so you wouldn't disturb her while she was shopping. That's the whole point. That's why she told me to drive you around." She insisted, "I want to see Auntie. I want to see her. Where is she?"

I said, "Okay." We rode around the street again, went into the parking lot, and parked. I explained, "Breanna, we're going to walk. Hold my hand. Now, when you see Auntie Angie, you can't run because cars are coming through, and it's dangerous. You have to hold my hand, and I'll take you across the parking lot." She said, "Okay, Uncle Damone." Well, I just knew when her little five-year-old self saw Lady Angela - her Auntie Angie - she would take off running. She held my hand, and then she tried to get away. But the reason she could not go wasn't that she was holding my hand; it was because I was holding her so tight that even though she tried to run and get away, I kept pulling her back to me.

That is what God's love is like. Even though you try to get away from Him, something keeps on drawing you back. Even though you tried to run away from Him, you tried to drink your way away from Him; you tried to drug your way away from Him, you tried to sex your way away from Him, nothing will separate you from the love of God in Christ Jesus!

Let us pray:

LORD, forgive us for our selfishness of the times that we start to promote ourselves with a sense of self-service, pride, and greed. Help us, LORD, to be mindful of others and to walk in the love that you've demonstrated to us.
In Jesus' name. Amen.

Chapter 12
THE THRILL IS GONE
Revelation 2:1-7

"Unto the angel of the church of Ephesus write; These things saith he that holdeth the seven stars in his right hand, who walketh in the midst of the seven golden candlesticks; I know they works, and they labour, and they patience, and how thou canst not bear them which are evil: and though hast tried them which say they are apostles, and are not, and hast found them liars: and hast borne, and hast patience, and for my name's sake hast laboured, and hast not fainted. Nevertheless I have somewhat against thee, because thou hast left they first love. Remember therefore from whence thou art fallen, and repent, and do the first works; or else I will come unto thee quickly, and will remove they candlestick out of his place, except thou repent. But this thou hast, that thou hatest the deeds of the Nicolaitans, which I also hate. He that hath an ear, let him hear what the Spirit saith unto the churches; To him that overcometh will I give to eat of the tree of life, which is in the midst of the paradise of God."

An older couple was driving down the street one day, and as they stopped at an intersection, they observed a younger couple in the car in front of them. The man was in the driver's seat, and the woman was sitting next to him and hugging him so closely you could barely see where one ended and the other began. The older wife in the rear car said to her husband, who was gripping the car steering wheel in his hand, "We used to be like that. We used to be close just like that." The husband looked at the wife and said, "I didn't move."

We often look at the relationship other people have with God, and it seems so rich, so real, and so refreshing. If we are honest with ourselves, many of us will say our relationship with God used to be close. I used to be serious about Jesus, or I used to have quiet time with God. You used to be the first one at Bible study or the first one at service. You used to look forward to worship, but it is not like that anymore. If we were to say to God, "We used to be like that," God would reply, "I didn't move."

Seven is the number of completion in the Bible. We get a complete look at Christ by studying the letters He told the Apostle John to write to the seven churches of Asia Minor. Every letter has a word for the congregation in general, but they also have a word for the congregant individually, which helps us in our individual lives.

Because the church is the Bride of Christ, this is the bridegroom speaking to his bride. It helps us in our relationships because it represents a groom, a husband speaking to his wife. If you are not married, it does not matter; this is still a word that can benefit you.

Modern-day Turkey is Asia minor. That is the area where the church of Ephesus was at the time. Ephesus is the first church John mentions. It was a port city known as a center for commerce and trade. Strategically located, there was a temple there for the goddess Diana, or Artemis in Greek.

There was a lot of commerce and exchanging of goods. It was a political city. Even though the Ephesians were under Roman rule under emperor Domitian, they were allowed to self-govern. There was a lot of sexual immorality in Ephesus. Artemis - or Diana - was the goddess of fertility. So Ephesus was known for fertility and finance. Sex and cash were the main commerce and primary sources of income in that region.

Paul went there and started preaching the gospel. You can go to Acts Chapters 19 and 20 to get a background on the start of the church. If it were in existence today, this church would have a Facebook page, a YouTube channel, and a website because it was serious about spreading the gospel. Paul started preaching in one place, one area - Ephesus - as you can see in Acts 19, but the Gospel spread all over Asia minor. They were serious about sharing the Gospel.

John the Apostle is writing a letter to the church of Ephesus, to its members from the Master. The letter starts with a characteristic of Christ. Christ gave seven different characteristics of himself in all seven churches and let us know that He gives us just what we need. Whatever we are in need of, Jesus reveals, reminds, or reviews that characteristic of himself.

He says he has the star, which is the pastor, in his hands. That is encouraging to me. No matter what comes my way, I know I am in the hand of Jesus! When he says he holds the stars in his hands, it does not mean he has a piece of the star, but the star is completely in His hands. The Father has placed us in the hands of Jesus, and no one can pluck us out of His hand! This world is crazy, but I am thankful that the song says, *"He's got you and me brother in his hands! He's got you and me sister in his hands! He's got the little bitty baby in his hands! He's got the whole world in His hands!"*

He is constantly, continuously, and consistently walking amongst the lampstands, which means He is always walking among the churches. He is qualified to speak about the church because He is right in the midst of the church.

In the Scripture, He commends them; then He condemns them; this is a constructive way to deal with people. Whether it is husbands and wives or parents and children, this is a good interpersonal way to deal with relationships. Start with something complimentary, and then give them a constructive way to correct whatever you bring to their attention. It is also a good way to evaluate work among supervisors and employees, commend or compliment, then give your critique and a constructive plan to improve or a way to correct.

He starts by saying In Revelation 2:2, *"I know thy works."* Sometimes you work in the church, and you do not get the proper recognition, but Jesus says I know your works. People may not know, but God knows, and one day He will say, *"well done thy good and faithful servant (Matthew 25:21)."*

This was a church that had *Duty* and *Determination*. They worked hard while they were going through tough times. They were waiting and working. Isaiah 40:31 says, *"But they that wait upon the LORD shall renew their strength; they shall mount up with wings as eagles; they shall run, and not be weary; and they shall walk, and not faint."* You need to be working. If you want a job, you need to be knocking on doors and sending emails. Work while you wait. If you are looking for a mate, you need to learn how to smile.

This church had *duty*, and *determination*, and it also had *disdain*. Jesus said, *"I know thy works, and thy labour, and thy patience, and how thou canst not bear them which are evil: and thou hast tried them which say they are apostles, and are not, and hast found them liars...But this thou hast, that thou hatest the deeds of the Nicolaitans, which I also hate."* They hated what God hated. They did not hate wicked people but wicked practices.

The Nicolaitans were a group that took spiritual liberty too far. They believed you could live any way you wanted, and God's grace would cover you. The Church of Ephesus understood what false teaching was because they knew the word of God for themselves. They were not fooled by a preacher who had a black suit, a giant cross, and a large textbook Bible. That does not mean he or she is real. You need to know the Lord for yourself. They knew who real apostles were and who were not. When they said apostles, they were not talking about the 12 Apostles. The reference is to a group of itinerant apostles who said they were apostles, but they really were not.

Now, after commending them, Jesus critiqued them. He said in Verse 4, *"Thou hast left your first love."* Basically, what he said is *the thrill is gone*. This church had duty but no devotion. They had labor but no love, service but no sensitivity. They had their hands in it because they were doing a lot of work, they had their head in it because they could distinguish right doctrine from wrong doctrine, but their heart was not in it. Do you go through the motions with no emotion? Jesus said, you are ministering and doing things in the church, but you are not doing it with love. He said you left your first love, which means you had it once, but you left it. Sometimes we get so caught up in going through the motions, doing the work, and doing the labor that we forget it is about love. It is about love for Christ, love for other believers, and love for those who are outside of the church.

In Ephesians 1:15, the Apostle Paul commends the Ephesians for their love. So, they had love at one time, and now it was gone, but when did they lose it? I suggest that they lost it over time. Typically, when people leave the church or leave Christ, it is usually not a blowout but a slow leak. You missed one Sunday. It's ok; there is another Sunday in the month. But then you miss another Sunday and another Sunday. And before you know it, you are out of the church.

When a husband says, "I want a divorce," he did not decide that that morning. A wife who says, "I'm leaving," did not decide that right at that moment. They arrived at that decision over time. You never want your relationship with God or your relationship with your spouse to get stale.

Finally, He gives them a constructive way to get it back and get it right: *Remember, Repent* and *Repeat*.

Remember
Think about how good your relationship with God used to be or your relationship with your mate or partner.

Repent
Change your mind and change your direction. Satan uses our past against us to make us think that if we stray from God, we can't get back. But if you turn around and repent, God will forgive you and receive you.

Repeat
Redo those things that you did at first. If it's in your relationship with your mate, remember how you used to date. Remember those acts of love you used to show your spouse; redo those things.

Let us pray:
LORD, we are so prone to wander, prone to leave. You are LORD that we love so much. Thank you for drawing us back to you through your love. Help us to never forget you. Rekindle the fire of sacred love in these cold hearts of ours. We pray this in Jesus' name. Amen.

ABOUT THE AUTHOR

Damone Paul Johnson is a recognized teacher, preacher and author.

He is the Senior Pastor of Metropolitan NTM Baptist Church in Upstate New York. As the lead shepherd for 17 years, his transformational teachings continue to thrive amongst the intergenerational congregation which has grown in ministry and mission. Under his leadership, Metropolitan expanded its footprint in its beloved community and shaped a virtual church ministering to people around the world weekly on Facebook, YouTube, and the church's website.

He is also the founder of DPJ Ministries, whose mission is to take the word of God to the world. The emphasis on Word and world, taking the Word - the Holy Bible - to the uttermost parts of the world.

He lives in Albany with the love of his life, his wife, Angela D. Johnson.

www.damonepauljohnson.com
Facebook: @dpjministries
Instagram: @dpjministries

OTHER BOOKS AND RESOURCES
BY DAMONE PAUL JOHNSON

A Life Worth Rebuilding
A Life Worth Rebuilding Study Guide

Beyond the Grave Devotional